I0452903

The Library of Distinctive Mystery Fiction

BESTSELLER
MYSTERY MAGAZINE

Including MERCURY MYSTERY MAGAZINE

WILDSIDE PRESS

The
Lady
Regrets
by James M. Fox

James M. Fox (James M. W. Knipscheer), is a Dutchman now living in California. Educated in Berlin and at Oxford, he came to the U. S. in 1937. During the war he served as Army Judge Advocate of the Netherlands Government in exile. A trained lawyer and accomplished linguist (he speaks six languages) Fox combines the literate plausibility of British mystery writing with the bone-snapping action and suspense of the Americans. The result is always sparkling reading—in this case an electric tale of kidnapping and murder against a California background.

book
reprint
feature

CHAPTER I

As far as i'm concerned, it never pays to speculate about the laws and principles of Fate, if any. The breaks come and go as they please, regardless, and you can't ever be sure whether they're real breaks in the first place or just phonies—things might have worked themselves out better in the long run without your so-called fairy godmother interfering in what looks like your favor, sometimes.

The way it happened that Tuesday morning did look like a piece of luck as nimble as a smart pickpocket's second finger, right hand. We'd slept pretty late; something like nine-thirty, which is good and late after you've got accustomed to years of army routine—it takes more than your first couple of weeks' terminal leave to overcome little things like that. Then it turned out that this Colchester Arms hotel had a restaurant all right, but they'd discontinued room service, even on breakfast. The hired help didn't like to bother, and customers were still a drug on the market; they couldn't afford to squawk, not in Los Angeles they couldn't, not in September, a.d. 1945. That was one for Suzy to handle; she has one of those telephone voices that can sell General Motors stock to a vice-president of the CIO. In ten minutes two waiters arrived with pitchers of orange juice and cream, pots of coffee, plates with fluffy scrambled eggs, four rashers of bacon apiece, hashed brown potatoes, country sausages, tomato sauce, French toast, cinnamon toast, hot rolls, six pats of butter, and a fresh pot of marmalade. "Good morning ma'am, morning Major! Yes, sir, sure looks like a nice day. Will that be all, Major? O.K., sir, thank *you*, sir."

So one grins, and one eats; after three or four years in Europe, it gets to be an experience, eating. Then one discovers one is out of cigarettes. The second cup of breakfast coffee without a cigarette tends to warp an otherwise happy outlook on life, we have always considered.

5

In this manner it came about that a little after 10:00 A.M. I slipped quickly into slacks, a shirt, and coat and went down in an elevator to the lobby on a simple, innocent mission for a pack or two of common, everyday cigarettes. Philip Morris, to be exact. Not that it made any difference.

The Colchester Arms was one of the smaller apartment hotels on Serrano off Wilshire in the Ambassador district. Our cabdriver had found it for Suzy and I, after we drew blanks at five other hotels the night before. The housing shortage had L. A. by the scruff of the neck; people were sleeping in cars, on park benches, and in terminal waiting rooms by the thousands. By comparison, the Colchester Arms was a very plushy caravanserai, a nice cool six-story square of yellow brick behind a little garden walk primly landscaped in hydrangea and potted palms. The lobby amounted to nothing much, just a blue rug and a few easy chairs standing around in it and a small reception counter with mail pigeonholes and a PBX in one corner. That was the corner where a short corridor cut off at right angles toward the dining room in the rear.

There were two elevators, with only one working, both on the corridor out of sight from the desk. The cigarette machine stood next to them, almost on the corner of the lobby; the place was too small

to afford a cigar counter. I stepped out of the elevator and over to the machine, gave it my money, and pushed on the prescribed buttons and things. My nickel and dime tinkled musically inside somewhere, the machine grunted wearily, clicked a couple of times, made a noise like a self-satisfied hiccup, and leered at me with its five neatly stacked rows of popular brands behind vertical glass windows. The metal slot at the bottom remained empty.

My left eyebrow went up, and I lifted one large but fairly shapely and well-preserved hand, made knuckles with it, and rapped on the Philip Morris window. Nothing uncouth, just a mild, encouraging little rap, a courteous little admonishment to deliver for value received. When this was ignored, I stood back and surveyed the situation for a second or two, deliberating with myself on whether to resort to more forceful persuasion or to submit a claim to higher authority through channels.

On such fatuous little decisions as these may hinge the most fantastic consequences.

Two weeks of terminal leave had made me soft. I took a step toward the lobby to seek an interview with the desk clerk in pursuit of alternative number two. The one step was sufficient to give me a side view of the desk around the corner and to make me pause. The clerk was busy.

Two men were leaning casual elbows on his counter, so close to me that I could have reached out and tapped the nearest shoulder. They looked pretty much alike and could at careless inspection have passed for brothers. Both were short, middle-aged, heavy set citizens with round, red, sweaty faces and receding, vaguely blond hairlines showing under their identical Panamas. Both wore wrinkled Palm Beach suits a size too narrow about the waist and baggy in the knees, and pointed maroon oxfords with a lot of fancy stitching. Where Mike had it over Ike, sartorially speaking, was around the neck, which sported a tie, rayon, brown-striped, conservative, complete with pin, Shriner's emblem, imitation gold, one. No tie for Ike, who belonged to the open-collar, or raw-meat, school of dressers.

I took another smaller step backward and stood with my back to the wall, just inside the corridor. I'm allergic to cops, period. Put a cop in with me, and it spoils my temper, curls my upper lip, and starts me sneering. The way they have of asserting themselves and throwing their weight about and their consistent, inveterate suspiciousness about everything and everybody make me break out in a purple rash almost on sight.

Only on this occasion it turned out to be something special.

The conversation came through to me very nicely, of course; but for the corner paneling we were almost in each other's laps. They had just come in, and they weren't up to much more than passing the time of day with the clerk. It didn't take long to come down to business. What, Mike demanded to know, was new?

Nothing much, in the clerk's opinion. Four yesterday and one early this morning. There was a light riffle of papers and a short-lived silence, cut off sharply by an interesting duet of imperfectly interrupted respirations.

"Well, forchrissakes!" said Ike. "Whaddayaknow!" He sounded mildly in awe.

"Yeah. Sounds like them all right," said Mike, not dubiously, more with a lick of pleasurable anticipation, as if he were hefting a billy and getting set to use it on a small boy. "Major and Mrs. John C. Marshall, Washington, D. C. Ain't *that* somethin'? They come in early this morning, you say? What time would that be?"

"Can't tell for sure," the clerk said uneasily. "Mr. Wilson's on duty nights. He gave them four-fifteen, we got a reservation on it from Salt Lake City canceled last night, made it our only vacancy. Nothing serious, is it, sergeant?"

"Naw. Nothing serious," said Mike, unctuously.

Ike released a fat little chuckle. Behind me, the cigarette machine sighed and gave another slight hiccup. I glanced at it and saw a package of Philip Morris peeping at me from the slot. I reached over and picked it up absentmindedly.

"Use your phone?" Mike suggested.

He named a Glenview number, and I could hear the ripple of the clerk's PBX dial. There was a moment's silence, and then: "Kennedy here. Yeah. At the Colchester Arms. Registered as Marshall and everything, cool as you please. Whaddayamean, ya don't believe it? Think I'm nuts or somethin'? I'm looking at the registration right now, Major and Mrs. John C. Marshall, Washington, D.C., it says here. Nah, we didn't make no pinch yet. The guy's a cinch to carry an iron. O.K., send the wagon, we'll stick around. Sure. Yeah, looks like they're still sleeping it off. OK, don't bust a gut, will ya, it's a setup." He slammed the receiver and snorted contemptuously.

I considered I'd had enough. The elevator was waiting almost at my elbow, the colored girl operator hunched on her stool, her nose buried in a much-thumbed copy of *True Romances*. She did not look up, just reached with one lazy arm for the controls and gave me a shot up to four. Our room was at the end of the corridor. I reached it in a dozen long strides, barged in, and locked the door behind me in one continuous movement.

"Quick, pussycat. We're travel-ing. Pick it up and throw it in. You have ninety seconds."

My little helpmate is quite a gal. One hundred and fifteen pounds of judiciously curved size-twelve young woman, with enough leg to make Varga's young ladies turn green, a reckless shoulder-length mop of sparkling auburn hair, and a pair of deceptively thoughtful silver-gray eyes that can tie you or anyone else up in knots by just looking. She's from way below the Mason-Dixon line but won't talk that way except for a fee of five bucks per half hour, cash in advance. I give myself an occasional treat and buy fifteen minutes' worth.

"Johnny, don't be funny. Did you bring them?"

"Bring who? Listen, baby lamb, I'm not kidding worth a damn. We're drifting, but fast. Get busy, will you!"

"Cigarettes, darling," she reminded me. She was still in pajamas, cobalt-blue satin ones with black lace trimmings, which made her look rather like a hussy and she knew it. She was curled up on the pillows, the picture of seduction but spoiling it by pointing at the pack of Philip Morris in my left hand.

I grinned dangerously and flicked her the pack.

"O.K., peachy pie. Have it your way. You stay right where you are, and have a nice long smoke. I'll go see about a lawyer. Maybe tomorrow he can get you out on bail, *if* the judge cares to set any."

That did it. Bail was the operative word. It has a flavor that gets them every time. She was up and at me in a flash.

"Johnny, what happened?"

"No time now. Just you snap into some clothes."

You'd be surprised if you knew just how quick a woman can dress and two small suitcases can get packed when the formalities are dispensed with. Ninety seconds may not have done it, but it was nice smooth teamwork all right. For once we were unencumbered except for only the elementary sort of stuff that a sensible couple takes along in the Pullman on a long journey, and our real luggage was still represented by a handful of Railway Express vouchers.

The Colchester Arms was one of those buildings that doesn't believe in taking chances, or maybe the owners liked to keep their insurance premiums down. All brick and steel, with two separate sets of built-in fire escape stairs, and lots of huge red arrows pointing the way all over the place. We were halfway down the back stairs when the thin dying scream of a siren found our ears through the walls. It was dead by the time we hit the basement, a hollow concrete affair with one dim electric bulb glowing in a corner and lots of old trunks and empty laundry baskets untidily stacked about. There were any number of doors to pick for an exit, and nobody to argue with about the principle of the idea—at least not yet. I picked one more or less at random. It was bolted on the inside, of course. Hotels worry more about people getting in than out these days.

The yard had only just enough space for a delivery truck to turn around in. It was empty and let us out on a back alley, hardly better than a rough strip of gravel, connecting with Oxford Avenue, the next street. Sunshine came down on us in hard white splashes between the quiet brown palm-tree umbrellas. The street was deserted except for a half-dozen assorted parked cars at the curb and a small blue and white bakery van crawling on its appointed rounds in first gear, the driver hopefully blowing his whistle after customers and getting none.

"Are you going to tell me?"

"You bet I am, luscious. Just keep on walking. Right now what we need is distance and a place to park these bags. They're not so heavy, but they do call attention. Any time now, this neighborhood'll start buzzing with cops. It's my own fault, of course. I should have known better than to let you talk me into falling for that Havers publicity gag. It looked like a screwball proposition from the start, and now it's turned strictly snafu on us."

"You're so mean!" she accused me, heatedly. "You know very well I didn't talk you into it. All the way from Kansas City you were bending my ear with how much you approved of the idea that here was at least one member of the idle rich ready to show a bit of real appreciation of what the army has done for them, and how smart Havers was at picking them when he picked you, and all about the valuable connections we'd made, and everything. Did you expect me to dare disagree with you?"

"Like hell you wouldn't, if you felt like it. Listen, let me think a minute, will you? We're in a big mess of some sort, and I've got to figure out how to handle this."

"But, darling, the police of all things. . . . Why are we running like this anyway, we haven't done anything. When they find out we skipped, it will only make it look worse, and the hotel will sue us for their bill and then we'll really be in a spot . . ."

"Don't worry about the hotel bill," I told her absently. "Paid in advance, paid the breakfast check, all clear and shipshape. It's cop trouble I don't want any part of. Not till I've had a chance to check up on it somehow."

We'd reached the Olympic intersection by then and rode a bus in silence for a couple of miles. I didn't know Los Angeles very well, but well enough to get around in it, and I knew we weren't going to get anywhere on our feet or in buses. We had intended to buy a car in the next few days, and it might as well be now.

"What are you going to do?"

That was on La Brea, where I'd made her get off the bus, and we stood before a drugstore window with our silly old suitcases, looking like honeymooners on their first quarrel. She had worked up half a gale of annoyance on the short trip. I put an arm around her shoulders and squeezed, grinning at her. I wasn't really worried yet. The whole thing was still mostly a game as far as I was concerned.

"Look, honey bunch, you take the bags and go have a coke in here. I'll be back in ten minutes with a present for you. Then we'll get to work on this and straighten things out, huh?"

I held the door of the drugstore for her, still grinning sweetly, and she hesitated and took the bags and went in, tossing her stubborn auburn curls out of her eyes. When she'd gone, I walked quickly around the corner and crossed La Brea to a used-car lot I'd noticed from the bus.

It was a large, well-stocked lot, and the salesman wore a shiny new discharge button and had ex-noncom written all over him. Maybe he could read ex-major across my stern-faced countenance just as easily, for he struggled visibly with the temptation to push off on me a gleaming '42 Buick convertible with one fender slightly darker than its mate and a queer little ticktock in the motor. I gave him a cigarette and a cocked eyebrow, and he broke down to show me a dusty old '40 Packard sedan on an off corner of the lot, with only 30,000 on the clock, and upholstery, pedals, rubber, and fixtures to back it up. The motor made no more racket than a carefully oiled sewing machine.

"That's more like it," I said, and started to feel for my wallet.

"Hell, it's the only heap on this dump worth a kick," he told me. "Sir," he added hurriedly, winking at me.

I grinned and paid him a bucketful of money, and inserted myself behind the wheel. Nothing is easier than buying a car in California.

At the drugstore, Suzy came running, her vexation almost forgotten, eyes wide and shining.

"Whee, a buggy on four wheels! Darling, it needs a bath! Did you buy it? How much?"

"Too damn much. Hop in, we're in a loading zone, I don't want a ticket at this point. This is transport, and it carries our luggage, and it sleeps two, if necessary. Now we'll go find us a quiet spot and a phone, and we'll call our pal Henry."

It wasn't as if I had anything against the guy. Mr. Henry Fleming had struck me as a fine upstanding young man who would go far and have a nice trip on the way. I didn't blame him for the events of yesterday. He was, after all, on the Havers pay roll, and from that point of view his original idea was reasonable enough.

The Western Union boy, a pimply, ferret-faced youth in sweat-stained slacks and shirt caught us at Kansas City: MAJOR JOHN MARSHALL c/o TRAINMASTER A.T.S.F. THE CHIEF 52 WESTBOUND. CORDIALLY. INVITE YOU AND MRS. MARSHALL TO SPEND YOUR TERMINAL LEAVE AS MY GUESTS OF HONOR AT RANCHO PRIMAVERA. ANXIOUS TO SHOW MY APPRECIATION OF THE ARMY'S GRAND ACHIEVEMENTS AND PAY TRIBUTE TO YOUR SPLENDID PERSONAL RECORD. PLEASE WIRE ACCEPTABLE COLLECT. REGARDS. WILTON F. HAVERS, LOS ANGELES CAL.

It was one of those things. I'd hit New York on the *Queen Mary*, August 25, and received my pretty crisp white walking papers at Fort Dix two days later. The next few days had been commonplace, as such days go—you eat, you drink, you make love, you are generally tickled to death. Comes the dawn, and with it you commence to remind yourself about the more practical problems of reconversion.

Like a good many characters at that stage of the proceedings, we found ourselves with a sockful of liquid savings and a lot of fancy ideas about how to put them to work for us and live the congenial life ever after. But one idea was at the top of my list: after four straight years of rain, fog, frost, and snowstorms, I was going to have me a decent climate if it killed me. After four years of Spam and Brussels sprouts twice a day, there was going to be plenty of T-bone steaks, fresh fruit, and vegetables around. California or bust. We'd spend my terminal leave there and prospect the market for our own special and inimitable brand of brains and *savoir-faire.*

On August 30 we boarded a train for Chicago with through reservations to the coast in our pockets.

In that sort of spirit, such an invitation is not lightly dismissed or conservatively appraised. The Western Union boy at Kansas City didn't give us much chance anyway. Our train was getting ready to pull out, and he was shoving a message pad and pencil into my hands. I grinned at him, shrugged my shoulders in surrender, and wrote: WILTON F. HAVERS, LOS ANGELES, CAL. UNWORTHY OF SUCH HOMAGE BUT GLAD TO ACCEPT. MARSHALL. The boy took my quarter tip and all but spat on it.

It must have been a case of his professional ethics prevailing over his normal instincts, because the message got through in time for a welcoming squad to meet us at Los Angeles Union Station when the Chief chugged in behind its mournfully clanging brass bell Monday afternoon around five. Six obvious newspaper vultures, four even more obvious camera stooges, a small knot of curious bystanders, and Mr. Henry Fleming, officer in command.

He was quite a hunk of man, matching my own six feet plus with a couple of inches to spare and with the build of a popular college athlete. His immaculate, expensively tailored coffee-brown gabardine blended impressively with the deep tan of his pleasantly arranged features, and he knew better than to hide his expertly groomed crown of rich taffy-colored hair under a hat. He smiled up at us with clear wide merry blue eyes while we hesitated on the platform of our Pullman; he knew the number of the car, of course, and he picked us out of the crowd with the calm assurance of a conjurer reaching for the white rabbits in his topper.

"Welcome to sunny California, Major! And you too, Mrs. Marshall, with Mr. Havers' compliments, if you please!" He executed a flourish from behind his back and thrust an enormous bouquet of tea roses and gladioli up into Suzy's arms. "All right, boys, here they are. We'll do it easy, won't we? Don't mind giving the press a few brief moments, do you, Major? I'm Fleming, Mr. Havers' P.R.C. Happy to meet you. Be swell to have you with us."

"Hold it, Major!" one of the shutter maniacs yelled. Flash bulbs were popping at us by the volley. "Just put one arm around the Missus, will you? Look into her eyes—yeah, that's it, hold it now —thattaboy, that did it."

"How d'you like California hospitality , Major?"

That was the first vulture, swooping in from three o'clock low. I climbed down to the platform, assisted my sweet little burden in following, turned a fairly straight face on the inquisitor, and said, "Overwhelming. Isn't that the right answer?"

Everybody laughed politely for two seconds flat, then everybody let fly with a drumfire barrage of silly questions. We just stood there, arms linked, smirking at them.

At this point, our stalwart Mr. Fleming took charge again by the simple expedient of holding up one large capable hand.

"O.K., boys, let's do it smoothly, shall we? Major and Mrs. Marshall want me to tell you they feel delighted no end to be here. They've never met Mr. Havers, but they've heard of him, and they've accepted his invitation in the spirit in which it was made, a spontaneous if modest tribute to the Major's own grand performance and to that of his buddies and of the men under his command. He just wants to enjoy a darn good and well-deserved leave, and we'll see that he has one. Right, Major?"

"You said it," I admitted generously.

"Your heavy stuff in the baggage car, Major?"

"There was a little mix-up in Chicago," I told him. "Be a couple of days before it catches up with us, I'm afraid."

"Hey, Major!" The sardonic voice chased after us from the rear, crackling with insinuation. "Can you tell us whose picture's on a five-C note?"

There was a burst of cackling merriment in support. I didn't pay much attention, and Fleming offered a good-natured chuckle.

"That Sam Levy, always the clown," he advised me. "Don't worry about your luggage, Major. You can give me the checks later, and we'll send for it when it gets in."

He marched us out of the station and up to a car waiting at the curb in charge of a large, impassive citizen tastefully upholstered in black whipcord and leather. The car had a long, sleek station-wagon body on a 1939 Rolls Phantom chassis; nothing ostentatious, just rosewood and Cuban walnut and navy-blue marocain, with the initials WFH in silver leaf not more than an inch high. It swept us through the Second Street tunnel and out Beverly Boulevard, weaving effortlessly in the maelstrom of Labor Day cocktail-hour traffic.

Our Mr. Fleming meanwhile gave us of his best. In many well-chosen words he drew our attention to the lovely California weather and to his own satisfaction over our prospective visit, reminded us urgently that he was Henry to us, and painted a glowing picture of the many comforts and pleasures the Boss had lined up for us. He had an offhand predilection for odd puns and impractical bons mots, throwing them carelessly away without any evidence of expecting approval. He was the hail fellow well met, Chamber of Commerce type, and he seemed a pretty decent sort anyway, under it all.

The Rolls zipped through Beverly Hills and bore west again on Sunset Boulevard, picking up speed now that the traffic lights were behind us. Golf courses and polo fields rushed by in a blaze of green glory. I began to feel at home.

"Look, Mr. Fleming, Henry, I mean," said Suzy, innocently. "You told those reporters we'd heard about Mr. Havers, but we haven't really, you know."

He smiled at her with a tinge of embarrassment.

"I deserve that, I do for a fact!" he confessed. "If you're in a job like mine for a while, you forget that there are forty-seven other states full of people. In this one everybody knows the Boss—we've almost come to the point where we think he is California, don't you see, although that's silly, of course. He's just, well, a pretty big man locally, owns a lot of land, buildings, hotels, oil property all through the state. Dabbles a bit in politics, too, but you know how it is, not much of a market for an old boy with all the bright young lads these days, eh? He's a grand guy, though, real trooper with a heart as big as a prize watermelon, easygoing, generous, devoted to the children. Pity Mrs. Havers is away on a trip. You'd adore her; she's a very fine woman and a great beauty."

The Rolls swung sharply to the right and swished up a narrow tree-lined side road. I caught a glimpse of the sign that said Lucerne Canyon at the intersection. It ran fairly straight into the mountains, without much of a grade to it; almost immediately the cliffs towered over our heads, and the trees disappeared.

"As for the kids," said Henry seriously, "there you have me. They're all right, mind you, both of them, just a bit wild and irresponsible. You and I wouldn't worry if they were ours, matter of a few words here and a good old-fashioned spanking there. If you ask me, all these kids that are born where there's a lot of dough start out with two strikes against them. That much is off the record between us. The Boss dotes on them, you know, so don't you ever breathe a word of this!"

"It's a tip," I told him. "This place of yours is quite a way out, isn't it? What's it like, a real cattle ranch or do you just play at it?"

"Just an estate. The buildings are ranch style, and there are more than seventy-five hundred acres, clear down to the beach, but most of it's unimproved."

Ahead, the canyon lost interest in itself and ran smack into an unco-operative mountainside, but to the left an asphalt driveway debouched through an ornamental wrought-iron gate between two tall granite pillars. The gate was open, and to each side a trim low double-wire fence ran off into the hills: nothing to stop a small boy, merely a line of demarcation and a modest sign proclaiming, "Private Road, Keep Out." The Rolls changed its whisper to a gentle hum and tackled the steep grade unflinchingly. The driveway serpentined around a hill, dipped into the valley, and climbed in carefully engineered zigzags up the next mountain. This hillside was obviously part of the show: it grew trees, grass, and flowers instead of sage and manzanita like its neighbors; it reared up head

and shoulders over the rest of the landscape. Near the top the driveway ran in a wide oval loop around a huge sloping greensward lined with young cypress, except for the western sector where the road broadened into a crescent of concrete plaza in front of the house.

Ranch style was as good a word as any for it. It had something like a fifty-yard front with two large wings; it was two full stories high with a porch and a balcony along the entire length and solid rock all the way, much of it covered with ivy that would have laughed at a bulldozer. This monster of a house just sat there on that hilltop with an air of everlasting eternity and didn't care peanuts who knew about it, especially us.

A spare elderly Negro in close-cropped, fuzzy white curls, black tied, and tails stood on the porch steps, awaiting our pleasure. I had a quick impression of entering the cool resonant darkness of a small cathedral, of much polished mahogany, brown railings, and oversize paintings; the hall was two stories high and ran the full width of the house, with light filtering in through just three narrow stained-glass panels in the front wall. The floor felt like square tiles with an occasional mile of tapestry. Our usher crossed it, found a back door for us, and let us out into the sunset.

CHAPTER 2

OUTSIDE was a patio—and what a patio! About half an acre of Mexican flagstone mosaic, half of it glass-enclosed, the other half wide open, with a view like some poor devil's last nightmare after he'd been lost in the Gobi Desert for a week or two. The hillside had been carved up into a long succession of landscaped terraces. It was pink with flowers clear down to the bottom, and the clean hiss of a hundred sprinklers argued with the steady burr of an army corps of lovesick crickets. On the second terrace down shone the cream and turquoise jewel of the swimming pool, with a small beach hiding coyly in the trimmed evergreens that lined a zigzag path to the main house and to a couple of redwood bungalows on the far left. Voices and the twang of rackets on a ball betrayed the tennis court behind more landscaped shrubbery to the right.

In the valley and halfway up the next hill, orange and avocado trees marched in dark tiered groves, planted and nursed with infinite care on soil where they had no business to be in the first place. Beyond, the grubby sage took over again, and the bare hills ranged away toward the horizon, where the Pacific glittered like slender silver ribbon, drowning the sun's crimson fire under a sky bursting with gaudy splendor.

The tall, grizzled, solidly constructed citizen who had been lounging on a padded deck chair with his back to the sun heaved himself to his feet and came to meet us with the prescribed smile of greeting curling the iron bristles on his generous upper lip. "Welcome to Rancho Primavera, Major. And you, madame!" He did a quick double take on the little woman, allowed the smile to reach his hard brown eyes, took his hand away from me, and gave it to her in a hurry. "An honor and a pleasure," he assured us earnestly, nodding twice to make it stick. His loud gruff baritone seemed accustomd to have itself understood, and no nonsense.

We both spoke our little oh-thank-you pieces in the accepted style. The boss took them in his stride and suggested we come right on over, join the party, and have a drink or two. He had everything arranged just so, more padded chairs, and little glass side tables loaded with cocktail snacks, and another colored boy standing by in a white mess jacket to superintend the portable bar.

One of the chairs served a slim dark girl in the middle twenties, who sat straight up on its edge, watching our approach with cool eyes hiding behind slanting, shell-framed glasses. She wore a trim yellow silk number, anxiously smoothed out over her knees, and kept her thin small hands folded in her lap.

"My secretary, Miss Renshaw," said the Boss. He did not quite shrug his shoulders.

Our Henry fussed us into seats, almost rubbed our noses in the caviar, and ran back and forth with the daiquiris. He passed the cigarettes, pointed out the bungalow placed by the Boss at our exclusive disposal, and kept up a running fire of commentary. He reminded me of that bombardier who took a kitchen sink along and pushed it out over Berlin. It made things easy, of course. We could afford to sit back, sip our drinks, smile politely, and let the clouds roll by.

This happy state of affairs didn't last long. I was accepting my second snifter when running steps and a sharp whistle came from the garden. Almost immediately a strapping great Dane bounded over the patio's balustrade, cleared the distance to us in two more silent bounds, and pulled up short with its muzzle about an inch from my face. It drew back a pair of loose black lips, growled, and showed me a set of fangs that would have made a Bengal tiger pause to consider. The growl didn't make much noise. Just one of those low, insidious belly rumbles signifying marked disapproval.

The event caused a certain amount of general consternation. Henry stopped talking in midsen-tence and sat still. Miss Renshaw caught her breath in a small gasp. The Boss choked a quick malediction and snapped, "Here, Khan! Down! At once!"

The running footsteps materialized in a short, weedy young man who came panting up the garden path in dove-gray slacks and sweat shirt. He wore his rich russet-brown hair brushed straight back down to the nape of his long neck; somehow the effect seemed to emphasize the flat vacuity of his features, moonlike to the point where he had almost no profile at all. The watery blue eyes had all the expression and character of those usually on display in a still-born calf. However, his agitated manner gave ample proof of distress. He waved and whistled.

The dog did not even look up at him. It allowed a trickle of saliva to drip through its teeth to my shirt and growled again, liking me less.

"For God's sake, don't move, Major!" Henry urged me in a chatter. "He won't attack you if—"

"Heah, Khan, you stop that, suh!" my little bride and helpmate cooed sweetly in the Alabama vernacular.

The big hound pricked up both ears so fast they clicked, cocked its enormous head at her sideways, and walked over to her in three steps. It looked her over for a brief second, sniffed at her skirt, then relaxed and lay down at her feet, dropping its muzzle in her lap with a short grunt of contentment.

"Well, I like that!" I said indignantly.

Consternation broke into hilarity around me. Even the colored bartender, who'd been quietly edging toward the nearest exit, had fun at my expense. The Boss roared and slapped his hairy stomach. The weedy young man came trotting, pumped my arm, giggled at me, and said he was Bob Havers and how did I do. He had a high, shrill voice, carefully drilled into affectation by only the best private tutors, and he smelled of excellent bourbon, plenty of it.

So this was one of the "kids" with two strikes against them, who needed a few words here and a spanking there according to our Henry. I looked him over without much curiosity. He was somewhere in the twenties and typically 4-F in build and complexion—a mild little man, who ought to have a fairly smart Pekingese to show him around, instead of Khan the Brown Bomber. I wondered what the other one would be like. I didn't have to wait long for the answer.

The tennis players were coming in, having run out of daylight. Quite a couple they made, too.

"Aha, there they are," said the Boss, bursting with joviality. "Mrs. Marshall, Major Marshall, my daughter Lorna Mae. And Mr. Marescu, who's staying with us for a few days. Had a nice game, dear?"

She ignored the question, without so much as a look at him. She glanced at Suzy and said, "Hello," sulkily, with half a scowl to back it up. I rose from my comfortable deck chair, and she inspected me briefly with coolly speculative pastel-green eyes, allowing her lips to relax, before she held out a small strong brown hand to me. She seemed about twenty, with a loose shingle of coarse chestnut hair, a short, voluptuously curved, wide-hipped body, and long, sturdy, heavily tanned legs. She was in a white sharkskin halter and shorts, managing somehow to give the impression that she'd just as soon do without them. She gave me another hello, not so sulky.

The Marescu boy was really something. He wore custom-cut white flannels and a supply of cow's feet that made him around forty-five. He had a veritable authentic wave in his pitch-black mane, though, with a set of sideburns way down to here, and a nose to worry an eagle, and a slim lissome waist to bow from. He picked up Suzy's finger tips with the air of a high-class jeweler about to make a sale, and kissed them audibly, gazing deep into her eyes, assuring her he was enchanted. He executed another genuflection for my benefit and wanted me to believe that I, also, enchanted him. Thereupon we all sat down and had another drink, in an atmosphere suffering from a certain lack of congeniality, to say the least.

The whole setup was funny as hell, I considered. Put eight grown-up people, moving in about the same social ranks, together in a group on a nice cool patio with a view, and give them cocktails—you're supposed to get a cozy picture. As it was, even our Henry grew discouraged. Only the Boss had himself a time, playing host to the little woman, putting on the loud cheerful he-man act, coaxing her to give him some more of that honey from Dixie stuff, while the Renshaw gal just sat there with her hands in her lap, looking down her nose. Bob Havers hunched in communication with his bourbon highball and with the Pacific on the horizon. Lorna Mae toyed with a dry martini, listened to Henry's tedious little jokes, disregarded Daddy's repeated attempts to enlist her support, and threw me an occasional fluttering eyelash. The Marescu lad tried pitching to all the ladies in turn, got no strikes, threw a couple of curves at me, saw me smile at them, and settled for a tentative pat on Khan's formidable neck. The great Dane, who had been peacefully asleep

on Suzy's feet, opened one baleful yellow eye and curled up enough lip to bare one glistening incisor. Marescu gave up quick.

After some twenty minutes of this I began to receive distress signals from my favorite gray eyes and decided on a relief expedition. Our Henry joined up with enthusiasm.

"Yes, sir, Major, sure thing. You bet. Can do. Excuse me, Mr. Havers, sir, the Major suggests that he and Mrs. Marshall might like to freshen up a bit before dinner and inspect their quarters. . . ."

Our Henry took us by the arm and led us gaily down the garden path. The bungalow called iteself Casa Romero, in the same style, and was otherwise all that might be expected. The living room had a log fire going in the brick fireplace and lots of pioneer furniture, Hopi rugs, and hunting trophies; the bedroom allowed for a big Mexican four-poster, our two suitcases, and not much else. The bath had it all, chromium, crystal brick, rose marble, and one of those trick showers that hit you from six angles, including the floor.

"Anything you want, folks, there's always the house phone," our Henry pointed out. "Then on the dial job beside it you're through to town. It's a private line, not just an extension, in case you have any business to take care of. Well, make yourselves at home now, see you anon, we will. Dinner at eight sharp, you know. Tiddley-ho and stuff!"

He disappeared in a cloud of dust and benevolence, and we sat on the bed and consulted each other with doubtful chuckles in chorus.

"Johnny, aren't they peculiar?"

"You can say that again, cupcake. No like, huh? Hell, I don't know, I guess we'll get used to them pretty soon. They've got some swell scenery here, and the catering department seems in reliable hands. What about this Havers guy? You figure he'll be hard to handle?"

"He's just a big blowoff," she said seriously. "Playing the gallant host who wants me to be sure he's still in there punching. Half the time he was trying to flirt with me, and the other half he just talked about his children— he's so terribly proud of them, and they seem such a couple of punks, don't they? I'm sort of curious about his wife, but he never even mentioned her. Henry's nice, though, don't you think?"

"Henry," I conceded magnanimously, "is a great little guy. I feel sorry for him, my heart bleeds for him, I don't want his job, but I think he takes the brass ring on this show every time. Leave us not worry about our Henry. What we ought to worry about is getting fixed up for a meal. I'm all hollow inside, and I need a bawth."

It was in the bathroom, just when I found myself having a good time with the trick shower, that the plaintive moans came to intrude upon my ears. They were in the company of a series of muffled irregular thuds, so as to approach more closely the performance of a hanging suicide drumming his heels. A hasty glance out of the window cleared up my doubts.

"Hey! Your boy friend's calling on you. Get rid of him, will you? His tail's knocking the front porch to pieces!"

The dining room was early Chippendale, with six tall silver candelabras of sixteen tapers each providing the only illumination. It occupied one whole wing of the main house, its level raised about three feet over that of the vast central hall that had admitted us upon arrival. The hall had a few lights on here and there, which made it appear even more pontifical than before; there were a few substantial tables, chairs, and divans standing around in it, but they didn't even try. By comparison the dining room was almost snug.

That colored major-domo knew his stuff all right. He managed the works with an inconspicuous efficiency that made my head swim when I watched him for more than ten seconds. The food was good enough for a caucus of French politicians; there were six different clarets, three hocks, and a vintage '33 Heidsieck with the crêpes suzette. I was beginning to gain a more mellow perspective of the whole strange business.

They had given us the seats of honor, on each side of the Boss, and my left-hand neighbor turned out to be a dry old codger in a wrinkled white pongee suit, who was introduced to me as one Mr. Earl Spencer and who thereafter addressed himself exclusively to the contents of his plate. This was all I needed to persuade me to do the same. The rest of the company automatically split itself into two camps of three members each. The Boss and his P.R.C, with my cheerful little earful between them to keep them happy, and Messrs. Marescu and Havers, Jr., attending to Lorna Mae, not too successfully judging by the continuous pouting listlessness of her expression. The prim Miss Renshaw was nowhere in evidence.

There was the inevitable dessert toast to the war hero who after covering himself with glory and living through years of sacrifice for such as we, had now returned safely to the arms of his charming spouse.

The sparks didn't start flying until we had adjourned to coffee and liqueurs on the patio.

At that, they were not such terrific sparks; there were just many of them. From the minute we had been served, and the butler had made his formal exit, all of us got mad at everyone else.

Poor, innocent old Spencer started it by approaching the Boss with a request for a few minutes of his time—he had a matter of some importance which he'd prefer to discuss with him at his instant convenience. The Boss said sorry, not now, couldn't Spencer see he was entertaining a lady? The lady demurred ever so carefully that it was perfectly all right; after all Mr. Havers really mustn't neglect his affairs for her. The Boss got excited, dismissed her protest with a gallant gesture, knocked over a coffee cup, and told Spencer to forget it. He did not put it quite so moderately. The Heidsieck had flushed his hard, sallow cheeks and impaired his vocabulary. I became suddenly aware of a curious stiffness in his left arm and noticed for the first time that the hand was covered by a tan leather glove.

Spencer didn't seem to mind much. He merely shrugged, finished his demitasse, and strolled away into the garden. Meanwhile, Lorna Mae was trying to engage my attention and refusing to be denied.

"I beg your pardon, Miss Havers. Rude of me, but I was daydreaming. My picture, did you say?"

"It's nothing, really," she assured me. She pulled over a rattan taboret and seated herself at my feet, leaving Marescu flat and turning her back on him. "I just said you don't look much like your picture, Major."

"Oh? . . .Don't I?"

I wondered where she could have seen a picture of me. There aren't so-many in circulation, thank the Lord for small favors. Marescu came over to stand behind Lorna Mae. He was puffing on a cigarette through a long gold-plated holder and seemed eager to join in our jolly little tête-à-tête.

"You know, you don't. Your pictures make you look thin, sort of wispy. Not the way you are at all."

Now there was more than one picture already yet. My opinion of the "kids" and their mental perceptions refused to improve itself. They seemed to get mixed up on things. I grinned vaguely and inspected the tip of my panatela. Nothing wrong there, drawing quite evenly and rendering satisfactory service.

"I guess I've picked up a little weight recently," I offered, for want of anything brighter.

"Come, come, *querida*," said Marescu, nastily. "The Major can hardly afford to sit here flirting with you with his wife looking on."

"That," I said, "qualifies you as a silly ass, but we'll call it the brandy and pass it by. Now why don't you run along."

He stood glowering over me for a second or two, couldn't seem to hit on the right answer, suddenly turned on his heels and walked off. He passed behind Bob, slapped him on the back and took his arm, coaxing him along. Lorna Mae said calmly, "You did that rather well. Luis is such a jerk. Do you want to see the garden?"

"That's quite an idea," I said. "Let's go see the garden."

We were halfway across the patio when the Boss sang out. "Lonny! Will you be long, dear? Better take a wrap, it's getting cool!"

He did not seem at all surprised when she went right on without paying the slighest attention. I decided they must have a system of hurting people's feelings, probably with a first and second prize at Christmas for the best over-all yearly efforts. People are funny. We crossed the first terrace and continued on the evergreen-lined gravel walk past the swimming pool until she led me down some narrow rocky steps that brought us to a small plateau, half covered with climbing roses on a trellis.

There was nothing wrong with the setting. It had all the props correctly lined up—lots of moon and stars, a mild scented breeze, a twinkling little fountain, more flowers than you could shake a stick at, even a nightingale on the job practicing its most difficult cadenza. My cigar was a trifle out of character here.

She didnt bother to take my arm or anything. She just stood there, a couple of yards away, still studying me through those lashes. I smoked my cigar and took in the scenery, not without approval.

"You don't like me very much, do you?" she asked me after a while, in a very small voice.

"Am I supposed to?"

That stopped her for a minute, but no longer.

"But why—Johnny?"

"Go on with you. What are you after now, a lecture? Or a mushy speech about how pretty you are, and how I'm dying to, only I'm scared? Look, sis, I'll give you a hot tip—any time you want to impress a guy, show him that you hit it off with your father first. Or he might get the idea you could be a little stinker and hard to please. Catch on?"

"Oh, yes," she said, almost childishly serious. "My father. It isn't that. You don't understand. It isn't that at all."

"O.K. You asked me. What did you bring me down here for? I like to neck as much as the next guy, but why pick on me, with at least two unattached males handy and Hollywood twenty-minutes' away? I'm not that good!"

This one opened her eyes wide. She was a picture, standing there with the moon doing things for her hair and her skin, and the sea-green dress undulating rapidly in the right places with her sudden fury. I had half a mind to make a pass at her just because. But she saved me the trouble by calling me a stupid idiot and running away fast in a flurry of rustling organdy.

I looked after her, shrugged for the sake of philosophy, and finished my cigar before climbing back to the patio. She wasn't there; but the patient Mr. Spencer had finally caught the Boss's ear, and Suzy sat ten yards away, listening to our Henry's merry prattle. Marescu and Bob were nowhere in evidence.

"Getting latish," I suggested. "Feeling like some sack duty, sugar?"

"Uh-huh. Should we say good night? Mr. Havers looks pretty busy."

"Don't you worry, folks," said Henry. "Papa fix. You two better get some sleep, what with the long journey behind you and all."

On the way down to the bungalow Suzy hung on my arm and kept looking up at the stars and sniffing the heavy redolence of the hillside's blanket of flowers. Once I leaned over and bit the tip of her nose carefully. By and large I felt fine, considering the world a messy business but being amply satisfied with my own personal share.

"Was she nice to you, darling?"

That much I had coming to me, of course—nothing of the Green Monster's growl in it, just a tiny good-natured little ironic meow.

"Well, you know me," I reminded her. "Always wanting to see what goes on. Didn't do so good this trip. You reckon I'm slipping?"

"Poor sweet. It's your five o'clock shadow, honey, for sure. You've had your bath today, and everything. . . . Wait a minute, let me try one."

He arms came up around my neck. For a while I lost track of time and space, as one will if suitably encouraged under auspicious circumstances. When I felt my legs back under me again, she was smiling up at me, provocatively contented.

"Mm—mm. No Johnny, it couldn't be your breath either. . . ."

I lunged at her, and she made me chase her all the way down to our front porch. By the time we made it into bed, we were both helpless with laughter. There's no use in attempting to explain. You understand about these things, or if you don't it's just too bad.

It must have been about half an hour later when the phone started ringing. We woke up almost together and for a moment stared blankly at each other in the semi-darkness before I could prod myself into getting up and padding out on bare feet into the living room, expecting an obstinate lush or a wrong number.

But the bell didn't ring on the outside line; it rang on the house phone, clamorously insistent.

"May I speak with Mrs. Marshall, please?" That loud, gruff, brass-hat baritone, only not quite so confident, somewhat agitated. My eyebrows went all the way up to a date with my scalp.

"Well, now, Mr. Havers, we've retired, you know."

He didn't bother to apologize, he just waited. I suppressed a strong inclination to hang up on him, put the receiver on the table, and went back into the bedroom.

"It's for you, pussycat. The Great Panjandrum himself. He sounds odd. Better see what's on his mind and get it over with."

She was already halfway down, swishing a kimono over her pajamas, her high-heeled slippers clicking angrily on the hardwood floor. I could hear her say: "Yes, what is it?" sounding snappy mad. Then nothing for a while, until she came on again with, "All right. I'll be right over," in a different voice.

She returned to the bedroom, looking upset.

"It's about Lorna Mae," she told me hurriedly, tying up her

kimono and grabbing a scarf for her hair. "He's just found her, on the swimming-pool beach. There's something wrong with her. He was phoning from the bathhouse. Wants me to come down and help."

I started reaching for my dressing gown, but she shook her head. "No, darling, I'll go. It's probably nothing serious. Look, were you on the beach when you left her?"

"Certainly not," I said indignantly. "And I didn't leave her anywhere. She ran out on me, for no good reason at all. Back to the house. I figured. O.K., you go and see about this while I get dressed, just in case."

She clicked out rapidly and tripped away on the gravel walk while I hunted for clothes and cigarettes.

Several minutes went by. I found switches for the porch light and the living-room chandelier, chain-smoked a couple of cigarettes, and strolled about the house in mild vexation. Suddenly I heard Khan barking furiously some distance away, and soon after the gravel crunched again under lightly running feet. She came bursting in through the screen door, slamming it behind her.

"For goodness' sake," I inquired mildly, "whatever's the matter with you? That dog been bothering you again?"

She stood facing me, breathing fast and looking nervous and disheveled. She was biting her lips, her cheeks were flushed, and her eyes narrow with puzzled resentment.

"Give me a cigarette, Johnny, will you?"

I gave her mine and watched her calm down a bit.

"It wasn't the dog," she said finally. "He got me out of it. Johnny, I don't want a scene, you understand? We'll have to leave tomorrow, but I don't want you to start a fight or anything. Promise?"

I didn't like that. I could see what was coming.

"Tricked you, did he?" I suggested, feeling my teeth coming together.

"There was nobody on the beach," she told me angrily. "I looked around for a while, and I was going back when he stepped out of the bushes behind the bathhouse—you know that stretch where it's very dark because the trees are older and close together? He didn't say anything at all, just went right aheac and tried to make like Charles Boyer. It was pretty disgusting, and he's awfully strong, for a man with one bad arm. We had this long ridiculous tussle, with me trying to argue with him all the time until I got ready to scream, and then Khan came charging at us through the garden, and he suddenly let go and ducked into the bathhouse. So I ran off home."

"Nice going," I said. "Good thing that dog's fond of you. It'll probably keep him treed all night, you can still hear it barking. You-'re sure that was Havers?"

"Of course I'm sure. It was too dark to see his face, but that left arm, and the way he smells—Russian Leather scent, of all things. He'd been in the pool, I think; he was wearing his bathrobe, the striped one we saw this afternoon, and a towel over his hair."

"Well it just goes to show," I pointed out. "This whole setup is screwy anyway. All these people here act like a bunch from the hop house, except maybe Henry. We'll talk to him early in the morning and have him arrange for us to check out quietly. You know, Suze, something's been worrying me ever since we arrived— you remember that guy who yelled at us in the depot, about the picture on a five-C note? You don't think he really meant to insinuate that we were being paid for staying here, do you?"

"But, Johnny, that's too silly! Nobody's offered to pay us a penny."

"O.K., maybe they were too smart to offer us money. Maybe this whole thing's just a cheap publicity stunt, and we're the suckers. Henry's job is public relations after all, nothing else. If it's like that, I could see more easily why Havers wouldn't have a

great deal of respect for us. You know what? I'm going to call that reporter right now and find out. He sounded like he's hep to all this."

The L. A. *Courier* had his number, and Wyoming 5508 rang about twenty times before the connection clicked in and the wire transmitted a noise somewhere between a grunt and a snarl.

"Sorry, Mr. Levy," I said. "You need your beauty snooze as much as I do mine, but I'd appreciate a word of advice from you just the same. What's cooking on this Havers deal that I ought to know about?"

"Who the hell are you?" he yelled at me.

"Who the hell did you think I was? Chiang Kai-shek?"

He paused to turn that one over and look under it.

"Oh, the tin soldier boy with the Dixie cheesecake," he diagnosed at last, with a sarcastic chuckle. "Whatsamatter, Major, ain't they treating you right? It couldn't be you'd have a story for me there, would you?"

"Now look, sport," I said peaceably. "We're not such big chumps as you might have reason to believe, but we've been out of the game for a spell. Deal us in again, will you please? What about that crack of yours at the depot this afternoon?"

"Aw, shucks, that was just a dig at that guy Fleming. Nothing personal, Major. We figured he ought to stake you at least five C's for the job. Fleming's O.K., knows his stuff, but that gag of entertaining a serviceman to kill a run of smear publicity don't sit so well with us. Heck, we let you off easy yesterday."

"So Havers hasn't been doing much good lately, has he?" I prompted him.

"Are you kidding? I heard you guys get to read a paper every now and then. Most of that tax stuff's been on all the wire services for over a year. Drew Anderson takes him apart every other Sunday in his column—Junior slips by the draft board, Junior's booked for hit-run an' keeps his license, Junior's dog bites movie star. Now the old lady's packed up in a huff, and still he figures to run for senator next year. You wanna take any more of this?"

"Thanks, sport," I said, shuddering. "That'll do me very nicely." When I got through, the back of my shirt was soaking wet.

"Better start packing, cherry pie," I directed. "This is even worse than I thought. We're moving out right now."

She watched me uneasily for a moment, nodded, and went into the bedroom. I called the Yellow Cab station in Santa Monica and told them to have a taxi pick us up at the dead end of Lucerne Canyon in half an hour.

CHAPTER 3

THAT WAS the cabdriver who found us a berth at the Colchester Arms Monday night, and that was how things came to a pass where, on the Tuesday morning, it seemed like a sound idea to call our Henry and find out from him why the Los Angeles Police Department had suddenly developed such a pressing interest in our bodies.

We drove out Whilshire Boulevard into Beverly Hills, where I found a parking spot and a convenient public phone booth in another drugstore emporium and rang the Havers estate. The Renshaw girl answered almost before my dial had clicked back on the last figure of the number. She said, "Mr. Wilton Havers' secretary speaking," in a quick high jittery treble, as if she expected the phone to spit at her.

"This is the Hollywood Chamber of Commerce," I said cheerfully. "I'd like to talk with Mr. Fleming, please."

"Oh . . . I'm sorry, Mr. Fleming's in a conference just now. Can he call you back, Mr.—?" She sounded relieved, but still uneasy and in a hurry to get rid of me.

"Micklejohn," I told her blithely. "Clyde P. Micklejohn. Better tell Mr. Fleming right away, I know he'll want to take this call.

An important private matter. I'll hold on."

She was hesitating, and I could hear her breath over the wire, coming a little too fast. Finally she said, "I'll see. If you can wait, please," almost whispering, and there was silence for a long time.

At last he arrived, breezy as ever. "Yes, Mr. Micklejohn, Fleming here. What can I do for you?"

"Hi there, Henry," I said sunnily. "Howsaboy? You alone?"

"Oh-oh!" he came back, fast on the trigger but apparently undismayed. "Yes, indeed, Mr. Micklejohn. Anything you want me to write down, or how shall we proceed? Naturally, Mr. Havers is very anxious to, uh, co-operate and follow your instructions."

"Co-operate, my eye," I said. "Just you tell me what in thunder you're up to now. Seems to me you're overdoing this publicity racket to a point where I'm getting all set to sock your boss with a nice little writ for damages."

That set him back on his heels. "But Mr. Micklejohn, you mean to say you don't— Excuse me, what was the information you wanted?"

"Cagey, huh?" I was beginning to get seriously irked. "Come on, smart guy, give! Whatever possessed you to sick the cops on us? You want me to come out and kick you in the seat of the pants, or are you as goofy as that whole bunch you're stooging for?"

He took only a few seconds to digest those kind words.

"I'm terribly sorry, Mr. Micklejohn. It seems there has been a slight, ah, misunderstanding. The situation is rather difficult here. If I could have a little personal chat with you, perhaps. . . . Would you and Mrs. Micklejohn be prepared to meet me at the apartment of a friend of mine, say in an hour's time?"

"A friend in a blue shirt with shiny brass buttons maybe?"

"Oh, no, nothing like that!" he assured me urgently, lowering his voice. "We shall have complete privacy, I promise you. Apartment twenty-eight at sixteen hundred Fitzroy Drive."

"Make it half an hour."

Half an hour was about the time it took us to locate the place and drive out there, a large rambling white stucco building out on the fringe of Westwood Village, all cluttered up with Moorish arches and tiled stairways, fancy sundials, and bronze cupids supervising the patio fountain. We circled the block twice before we talked each other into parking the Packard across the street in front of a filling station. The neighborhood looked like quiet harmless middle-class. We went on in and found apartment twenty-eight in the rear of the building.

He was there all right, a bit tense and his merry blue eyes

guarded, but otherwise the same old Henry with the bright smile and the glad hand. He pulled the front door wide open from under my knock and let us into a pleasant sunken living room, chintzy and cool and shady with all the venetian blinds drawn.

"Come in, folks, come in, please. Glad to see you. Do sit down, won't you? May I take your coat, Mrs. Micklejohn? Thank you so much. Now, if you'd just give me your side of the story, I'm sure we can clear up all of this trouble in jig time."

We sat on the davenport together, giving him the stony stare.

"See here," I said, "fun is fun, but suppose you cut out the gag names and attend to the giving yourself, fella. Keeping in mind we could be peeved with you."

"Gag names? But sure, Mr.—"

"The name," I reminded him patiently, "is Marshall. Remember us? Major and Mrs. John C. Marshall. Now go on from there. Serve it with mayonnaise and a dash of angostura. All about that fat-faced boss of yours, who fakes his income tax returns and pulls strings to get his zany kids out of jams, and who makes elaborate passes at a guest while his wife's fixing to divorce him, and still he wants to be a big shot in politics. All about the cops, too. You might start with that part of it."

He'd lost several shades of tan by now, and he was groaning.

"Oh, suffering shades of Jehoshaphat! Are you serious, Major? Oh, Lord, what a mess! And your middle initial—it's C, is it? On the level?"

I was beginning to see the light. I pulled out my wallet and showed him my army card and driving license. His groan changed tune to a wail of agony.

"Thank God we've kept it out of the papers so far," he managed fervently.

"Out of the papers? Now I know you're a screwball. What about that riot in the depot yesterday?"

"You don't understand," he told me earnestly. "There's been a kidnaping. Lonny. Last night!"

Suzy gasped, and I sucked in my breath sharply.

"Not so good," I said, thinking very quickly. "You're sure it was the real article, nothing flimsy like boy friends?"

"No, sir, Major. There was a ransom note, and she'd put up a struggle, and there's all kinds of evidence. Most of it against you!"

"Now that's nice," I admitted. "Let's have it. I can hardly contain myself."

He stopped pacing the floor, dropped limply into an easy chair, and stared at the floor while he reeled off the story in a weary monotone.

"She'd told her maid last night to wake her up at seven. She had a date with Mr. Marescu to go riding before breakfast. The maid found her room in disorder, and the note on her bed, newsprint cut out and pasted on a piece of our own stationery. It's a short one. Here it is, if you want to see it. I copied it."

I took the note from him and examined it. It said: "Havers, keep your shirt on, she's okay, get 250,000 ready today in twenties tens fives, you'll hear from us, no cops or else." That was all.

"Mr. Havers was terribly upset and got in touch with one of his friends, who happens to be politically influential in the county. We all got together, with the Sheriff and a couple of deputies, trying to decide on a course of action, when around eight o'clock a telegram came in from New York City. You can read it yourself."

He gave me the wire from his pocket. It was a Western Union night letter with Monday's date stamp, dispatched from New York at 6:25 P.M. to Wilton F. Havers, Los Angeles, California, and signed John R. Marshall, Major, AAF. PRESS REPORTS STATE INACCURATELY THAT MRS. MARSHALL AND I RECEIVED AND ACCEPTED INVITATION TO SPEND LEAVE YOUR CALIFORNIA RESIDENCE. OUR WESTBOUND RESERVATIONS TAKEN BY IMPERSONATORS HERE AUGUST 30. ARE STILL AWAITING TRANSPORT. SUGGEST INVESTIGATION FOR YOUR PROTECTION.

"That damned booking office clerk at Grand Central," I said, grinning uneasily. "He had a cold, and he didn't make sense. I wondered at the time how he managed to have it all cut and dried for me—figured we were lucky picking up a cancellation. So you were really after the famous flying Marshall, were you, Henry?"

He nodded miserably, and I almost laughed at him. No wonder little Lonny had worried about how much I didn't look like my pictures. I'd never met "Buzz" Marshall, the hot-shot fighter boy of the E.T.O., but he was said to be quite a character, with more fruit salad than General Patton on the heaving bosom.

"And you started bragging about it to the newspapers, the minute you had my wire from Kansas City, accepting. O.K., so I can see what came next. We're impostors, and we've disappeared."

"There's more to it, Major," he told me. "It was an inside job, according to the Sheriff. No locks broken, no sign of a ladder or anything like that. And the dog wasn't disturbed. And they found a fresh cigar stub in her room. One of Mr. Havers' own panatelas, they're only offered after dinner. We checked and located every stub of those that had been smoked last night except yours."

"Uh-huh. Well, mine's supposed to be in the garden, near the pergola. What of it?"

Suzy broke in impatiently. "Darling, it's easy. Look, they figure like this. We're New York crooks, and we have inside information that they're going to invite the wonder boy Marshall. We finagle his train reservation, and we drift in with the tide. I handle the dog, and you play up to the gal. You have her show you the garden, and you make an assignation with her for later on. Then she lets you in, and you tie her up, and I come in, and we carry her out to the car. Only we didn't have a car then."

"You stole one," said Henry, grinning wryly. "There's a convertible Cadillac missing from the garage."

"Well, this is great stuff," I conceded. "And so now you have the Sheriff and the P.D. and the F.B.I. running us down all over L. A., while the real heavies are taking it easy and marking time until the pay-off. I like it."

"Only the Sheriff's office," he said. "They've been making a routine check of all the hotels and places. Just before you called me we had a report you'd been staying at some hotel downtown, but you disappeared before they caught up with you. Now they're sure you're it, you realize that, don't you?"

"And you're aiming to keep all this out from under the great American press?" I inquired incredulously.

"Oh, yes, we will, if we possibly can," said Henry, with much enthusiasm. "The Sheriff's promised to sit on it, and we've now decided to follow instructions and pay the ransom. It's been done before, Major, lots of times. Mr. Havers is frantic. He'd pay a million if they asked for it."

"You don't say! And where do we come in on this deal? I'm in a good mind to go see that sheriff. The way you have it, he'll throw us in the can but fast, and everybody will be tickled pink, figuring it's a cinch to make us tell where we've concealed the body. Then in a couple of days it turns out differently, and we can sit back and sue for a fat slice of that million on false arrest, libel, defamation of character. The *Courier* will love that. I can see Sam Levy licking his chops right now."

"Major Marshall, please! For God's sake, have a heart! You don't realize . . ." His voice stranded on a croak.

"Huh," I said. "Forget it. They brought me up a sissy. I'll play it nice. What's your idea for handling this?"

The little woman pulled at my arm restlessly.

"But, Johnny, the police. . . . We'll have to go to them; don't you see how dangerous it will be if we don't?"

"But you mustn't!" Henry pleaded, recovering himself. "They'd have to arrest you, and everything would have to come out. It would ruin the Havers family; it would ruin you, too, the publicity would, whether you sue or not—you know what employers and the public are like, the notoriety would mark you for life. And the real kidnapers might scare and kill Lonny when they find out the police are in. Look, I could let you have this apartment until the case breaks. It belongs to a friend who left on a three months' trip to Mexico last week. He always lets me use it. You can stay under cover here, I'll get you groceries twice a week, there are plenty of books, the radio, everything. And if anything happens I can square you with the authorities for hiding out, tell them it was my idea."

"You didn't mention to the Boss you were going to meet us here?" I asked curiously.

"Oh, Lord, no! You don't know how upset he is. He'd have come barging in on you with a shotgun. I promised you this would be strictly private, didn't I?" he added naïvely.

"Yeah. You did, for a fact. O.K., we'll duck the Sheriff, and we'll use the apartment, but no dice on that hiding out business. We can take care of ourselves. I used to be with army G-Two, m'boy, and that's a rough outfit; they show you things. And little Suzanne here has been around. We might even see if we can find the lady ourselves."

"Well, Major, it's awfully kind of you, of course. I'm sure your experience would prove very valuable, but you'd be taking a pretty heavy risk, you know. After all, you can see how it is. . . ."

"That's just it," I pointed out. "We can't. You're the guy who knows all the answers. That boss of yours is queer, he is. Did he happen to tell you about a little incident that occurred last night by the swimming pool, which accounted for our hasty departure? I bet he didn't!"

This worried him visibly, but he had to confess he didn't know, so we told him the story in words of one syllable. We had him wincing through it all and holding onto his head with both hands.

"This is getting worse all the time," he said at last. "I should probably have warned you, Mrs. Marshall—Mr. Havers has always been rather, uh, impulsive. There have been, uh, incidents before that I've had to cover up. I want you folks to believe me, though," he continued, warming up to his subject, "that the Boss is fundamentally a grand guy, who means well—wouldn't harm a flea, adores his children, generous to a fault, straight as a die in business. Most all of his troubles result from people taking advantage of him.

"I guess you've heard about Bob's bout with the draft board and his accident last spring. Bob's a congenital imbecile, quite harmless really, doesn't even show it most of the time. Naturally we don't want to advertise the fact. He wanted to go into the service as much as he ever wanted a thing, and he fooled his board into passing him 1-A, before Mr. Havers had even heard that he'd received a summons. We had no option but to pull a string or two —satisfied the board physicians all right, but the newsboys came down on us like a ton of bricks, and the Boss had to choose between his publicity and his family pride. I can go on like this forever, there's such a lot of it. But you understand now why I try to create a bit of decent publicity for the Boss every once in a while."

"What about Mrs. Havers?" I inquired dryly.

"Oh, she's all right," he told me, turning on a fresh dose of the boyish enthusiasm. "She's quite a beautiful woman, you know, excellent family, good taste, clever— it used to be such a splendid marriage, but sometimes those things just won't last, and we might as well face it, she became discouraged about Mr. Havers' occasional, uh, impulsiveness. Couple of weeks ago, she went off to live in Pasadena for a while, told Mr. Havers she wanted some time to herself to think things out. From the day she left, the gossip columns and the society pages grabbed it and made it sound like they were as good as divorced. We've come to expect it that way; all I can do is try. And now this terrible affair right on top of it all."

"Have you told Mrs. Havers about it?" Suzy asked.

"Not I! God knows how the Boss will manage, but it's up to him, I feel. It'll be a terrible shock to her. Lonny's her favorite; they were almost like twin sisters together. He might decide not to tell her, hoping he can make a quick ransom deal with these crooks and get Lonny back safe before she has to hear about it."

"Yeah," I scoffed, "a swell pair of fixers and deal wanglers you two are. You should have had the F.B.I. on the job from the first minute, bearing down hard. Those are the sports with experience in the snatch racket; they might even have the poor gal extricated by now."

"I suppose so," said Henry, unhappily. "He was all mixed up, at first, but now I'm sure he'd rather pay and not take any chances. The bank's sending the money over to him after lunch. There'll be a big suitcase full of it."

"You impress me, laddie. Now tell us some more about how it happened. What time did the Sheriff figure she was taken?"

"They didn't get much on that. She went to bed at eleven-thirty, the maid says—that was when she asked to be called in the morning. Nobody heard a noise or anything. I have a room on the same floor myself, and I slept through it. So did Bob, who is next door to her. The chauffeur had the evening off; he came back at two and noticed the Cadillac was gone—of course he thought nothing of it at the time, any one of us might have taken it out to go somewhere."

"When did you retire? And the others?"

"Just a few minutes after you two left the patio I went up to my room, read a magazine for an hour or so before I dozed off. Bob told us he took a short walk with Mr. Marescu and saw him to his bungalow. He came straight back and went to his room before I did, about ten-thirty he thinks. Margaret Renshaw was indisposed and upstairs all evening, had supper in bed."

"What about this guy Spencer? Who's he?"

"That's Mr. Havers' personal attorney. Duane, Spencer, and Morrow, they've represented him for thirty years. He left right after you did and went home."

"And the big noise himself?" I ventured. "Did he give any sort of an account of his movements?"

"Mr. Havers told us he spent some little time in his study after Mr. Spencer's departure and went straight up to bed from there," Henry said uncomfortably.

"Uh-huh. Well, it looks like they took her between twelve and one, while the dog had him cornered in the bathhouse. There's the irony of fate for you. I hope he's smart enough to have figured that one out for himself, including the poetic justice effect, using his daughter's name for bait in his silly experiment in amorous dalliance at that particular time."

"Darling, it's too pat, don't you think?" suggested my helpful spouse. "Almost as if they'd arranged the whole thing, to get the dog out of the house?"

"Now, Mrs. Marshall, really!" said Henry, staring at her. "You're not suspecting Mr. Havers of helping a gang of criminals to kidnap his own daughter and hold him up for a quarter of a million, are you?"

"I just thought they might have been terribly clever and have someone impersonate him," she explained. "After all, such a coincidence. . . ."

"No, that was the Boss all right," Henry assured her. "I don't like to say it, but that's just the sort of thing he'd do after a bit of a session with the brandy decanter."

"I wonder how he got out of that bathhouse," I said thoughtfully. "He must finally have talked Khan into putting up with him. The joke is that he probably saved the dog's life; they'd have a steak sprinkled with cyanide or something equally sudden on them. Those boys didn't come unprepared, they'd cased the joint. Had a finger guy in there, I'll bet. Could be the Marescu chappie, he's just the type. . . ."

"Really, Major, it would be so much better for you not to worry about this any more, in your own interest. If Mrs. Marshall and you will just sit tight here until it's all over. . . ."

"I told you, that's out!" I said firmly. "Now you listen to me, Henry. Go on home and play your cards, the way they want you to. Don't you fret about us, we'll make out O.K. But the minute there's any kind of a new development, phone us here with the full details. I'll require your word for it that you will do this, otherwise there's nothing in it for us but to see the police immediately. Of course, if Havers decides to have the Feds in after all, that will satisfy me, but until he does that, I'm not going to sit here on my fanny and let myself be framed up some more. Is that clear now?"

He hemmed and hawed a bit, and then he broke into a smile and shook hands with us, and said it was a fair deal.

CHAPTER 4

WHEN the sound of our Henry's footsteps had dwindled down the corridor, Mrs. Suzanne Marshall fixed a pair of balefully reproach-ing gray eyes on me. She fished a cigarette out of her bag with one small capable hand that didn't seem quite so steady as usual, and waited patiently for me to serve. I hastened to oblige with a light and with my best attempt at an enigmatic chuckle.

"Johnny, *honestly,* you're the limit. When are we ever going to settle down to a sensible kind of life and quit playing these reckless games you're always getting us into? You *know* it's mad not to go to the police at once."

"Oh, stuff," I said cheerfully.

Just the same, the whole cockeyed mess had me in a mental frazzle all right. The more my determination to crack it increased, the more I worried about methods and tactics. If only we could visit the Havers estate, look over the premises, interview the natives ourselves, we might get somewhere —as it was, we had to be satisfied with Henry's grudgingly supplied secondhand facts, and they were very far from satisfactory to me.

However, I was counting on the engineers of this pretty affair to provide us with our best chances when they got around to making an effort at collecting the bundle. And Henry had pledged himself to tip us off there, discreetly but efficiently. We had Henry over a barrel, and no fooling, I considered, he'd play ball or suffer to see his beloved reputation as a fixer blown to holy Jerusalem.

There was that finger-boy business. I bit off a chunk of liverwurst and Swiss on wholewheat toast, pulled over the phone, and dialed the *Courier*. Mr. Samuel Levy pounced on my wire quick as a woodpecker, and just as chipper.

"Howya, Major, what perks?"

"Right now I could use some information. You ever heard of a Hollywood character who calls himself Luis Marescu?"

"Sure, we know him, if you mean the director. Used to be at Globe, free-lancer now. Says he's invented a new color stereoscope; Havers is interested in it. What's he to you?"

I popped a slice of tomato in between the busy choppers and said, "Hmpf. I'm just curious. Gimme some more—a personal description, financial standing."

"Aw, the fancy-Dan type, movie wolf, lots of swankeroo. Been a local fixture for twenty years; Globe brought him over in the twenties from Europe—he was born in Rumania or some place. Tall dark slicker, long flossy side whiskers, very condescending. He should be pretty well fixed for chips, but I'd keep the Missus on ice if I was you, Major. Mister Marescu has one of those reps."

"Thanks, Sam," I said. "That'll do it. See you anon."

"Hey, listen!" he shouted. "Where can we get in touch with you? The city ed wants to—"

I gave the rest of it a miss, fin-ished my second sandwich, and made a grab for my hat. Suzy reached out and hooked one finger in a pocket of my sports jacket.

"Darling, you're not going anywhere special, are you?"

"Nope, nowhere special."

She came to back me up against the kitchen table, with her frown firmly established again and open for business.

"Where, Johnny?"

"O.K., now look," I explained patiently. "We've been all over this before. I'm not going to stick my neck out if I can help it. All I'm after is a bit more background information, and besides, I've had an idea where we can buy us some extra insurance against this deal backfiring into our pretty faces. Nothing flashy, merely plain old common circumspection."

"Why can't I go with you?"

"The phone, cupcake. Remember Henry? Some news . . ."

"Uh-huh." She stood up on her toes, kissed me quickly and turned away. "Be careful, honey," she said, studiedly casual, and walked out into the bedroom.

I hesitated for a second, slapped my hat in place, and went out. The old Packard grunted eagerly at a touch on the starter button. It found Wilshire Boulevard for me as if by instinct and kept up a smooth, contented hum of power for the half-hour trip downtown.

We parked on a Hill Street lot, and I walked a block to the Doheny Building on Pershing Square. The tenants' index listed Duane, Spencer & Morrow, Attorneys and Counselors at Law in suite 300.

One of the six bronze and copper grillwork elevators took me up to the discovery that suite 300 meant the whole third floor. The corridor in front of the elevators had been widened into a large stuffy anteroom, occupied by two motherly old ladies in severely funereal black—one behind a formidable reception desk in the center, the other in a corner cubicle serving the PBX. There were a hundred yards more of corridor on both sides, like a flat U, with any number of firmly closed doors on it.

"Yes, sir?"

The carefully pitched, noncommittal welcome to the lad who's not a client and who could be the Fuller Brush man. I selected expression number sixteen, Bewildered Stare, Ingratiating Type, and said, "Oops, sorry. Wrong number, I'm afraid. Looking for Waterbury and Company. Where is it, please, ma'am?"

"Are you sure you're in the right building, sir? I don't believe I've seen that name here."

I went back to the elevators, pretended to ring the signal, turned around and executed number twenty-three, Winning Smile, Slightly Embarrassed. "Excuse me, ma'am. Would there be, er, a gent's washroom here?"

That tickled her. Most of them are like that.

"Why, yes, I'm sure we have one. Just for the staff, really, but I guess it'll be all right. It's at the end of the hallway, you'll find the door easily, sir."

I found it all right, also two other doors, solid oak instead of frosted glass. The other doors said, "Mr. Earl G. Spencer," and, "Mr. Earl G. Spencer, Private." I tried the last one very carefully. It wasn't locked, and the baize-covered double behind it didn't seem to be either. I stepped quickly inside, let the doors sigh shut behind me, and walked around the big mahogany executive desk.

He did not seem particularly surprised. Not a muscle moved under the tight dry parchment of his cheeks, and the bright little red-rimmed eyes remained expressionless, almost disinterested.

He did not touch the papers I pushed across the desk. He merely glanced at them and allowed his eyes to relax a little.

"Yes, this would appear to be your picture. I gather that you mean me to envisage an unfortunate coincidence of circumstances involving a matter of mistaken identity. I may say that some such possibility had already suggested itself to me, and that I made reference to it when my client consulted me this morning."

"Oh, did you? I'll bet he liked it."

"For an innocent man," he dryly pointed out, "you seem to be remarkably well informed."

"Mr. Spencer," I said, "my wife and I did not kidnap Lonny Havers, period. But the way the land lies, we're very much concerned with finding out who did. We could establish our innocence by the simple expedient of surrendering to the sheriff and spending a couple of days in physical discomfort while he checked on our story. As it is, I'm more interested in handling this my own way. When these boys picked on us to carry the ball for them, they bought a packet, I'll tell you that much."

"Perhaps you'd care to sit down and tell me a little more," he suggested, still without much of a show of curiosity.

I sat and gave it to him, all of it, up to the minute we checked out of the Colchester Arms. He listened, never so much as moving one corner of his thin hard lips. He'd be blue murder in a poker game, he was such a cold customer.

"It would appear that you find yourself in a somewhat unusual predicament, Major," he commented, bestowing my rank on me for the first time. "However, I am inclined to put a certain amount of faith in your ability to cope with it. Your reluctance to sur-

render to the authorities I can appreciate, although if you were to consult me as an attorney, I should have to advocate surrender in your own interest. But I gather you did not come to me for advice."

"Information is what I'm here for," I said frankly. "You know now what my intentions are, Mr. Spencer. You can refuse to help, naturally. The way I look at it, your client will benefit if you assist me. Lorna Mae was kidnaped by smooth operators with an inside track. That means there are inside clues to be found. Is there anything that occurs to you along those lines that could be followed up?"

He kept his pensive gaze on me without ever wavering, as if he were lost in contemplation of some very abstract and austere problem in higher mathematics. I was commencing to grow kind of restless and impatient with him.

"What about the circumstances surrounding Mrs. Havers' decision to leave?" I pressed. "If there is another woman involved, the answer might easily be somewhere in that direction. It's worth considering anyway. . . ."

He pursed his lips at me on that one. It surprised me he could.

"Major Marshall, I am going to make you a most unusual, ah, offer," he stated placidly. "The situation is an extremely delicate and unhappy one, needless to say, and I am profoundly dissatisfied with Mr. Havers' reactions to it, much as I understand his present inability to form a sound judgment of its merits. Entirely apart from the elements of personal tragedy involved, this may affect the interests of stockholders in certain corporations associated with Mr. Havers' business enterprises, if there should be an open scandal with all the results thereof. My firm carries a responsibility to protect these corporate interests, and we have been discussing the idea of engaging the services of a private detective agency to assist us in such protection. It is only because discretion is to such an extent of the essence in the matter that we have so far refrained from taking this action. However, in view of your extraordinary status, and since you succeed in impressing me as a man of integrity and ingenuity, I should like to retain your services, quite unofficially, of course, and let me hasten to say wholly without prejudice to your rights and privileges under the laws of equity. I am prepared to suggest a fee of one thousand dollars and a bonus if you are successful. A very substantial bonus."

"Let me get this straight," I said. "You want me to get the girl back, if possible without benefit of ransom or scandal, and step on this snatch mob. You'll slip me some unofficial cash for that on behalf of Havers' corporations. In other words, if there are any kicks you'll deny you hired me or even saw me at any time, is that it?"

He nodded at me, gravely expectant.

"In a pig's ear!" I snapped at him scornfully. "I am not worrying about my rights under equity, Mr. Spencer, but anybody who thinks to hire me will take the consequences and like them! If this game blows up under my feet, you're going to stand up and say I came in here, and you trusted me and gave me the job."

He had his checkbook and a visiting card out and was writing while I made pretty speeches. I watched him with my eyes round and bulging uncomfortably out of their sockets. The check was for a thousand on his personal account; the card said: "Confirm retaining Major John Conger Marshall as of 3:00 P.M. today to investigate Miss L. M. Havers' kidnaping and all related matters, L. A. Sept. 4, 1945, E.G.S."

"Unfortunately," he observed calmly, "I can do very little else for you. I must agree that there are aspects to this case that appear to indicate the complicity of someone intimately acquainted with the Havers' family, but I have no facts of value to support any specific suspicion. As to the circumstances governing Mrs. Havers' departure, they are disturbing, but I am unable to discern a connection between them and the matter in hand."

"She wants a divorce?" I asked, halfway curious.

"Yes, I am afraid so. I may say this disaffection in a marriage of eighteen years' excellent standing gives me cause for regret. It is a different matter when these fly-by-night affairs break up—"

"Eighteen years?" I interrupted him, mildly astonished. "Should be longer than that, shouldn't it? The children are both in their twenties, after all."

"Lorna Mae," he countered dryly, "became seventeen years of age last month. Robert is thirty-one, and the first Mrs. Havers passed away in giving birth to him. Tragedy has always found a ready home on the domain, Major Marshall. 'Fate harries us, we answer not a word,' as the poet has it. I fear that it will be difficult to avoid a certain amount of deplorable notoriety in this case, with my client determined not to consent to a divorce, all the more so since he is under the impression that Mrs. Havers may be temporarily infatuated with another man."

"Is she?" I inquired bluntly.

"Perhaps so. Her name has often been linked with others, by those who make a point of observing such things for the public prints. To my knowledge the marriage has been good until fairly recently, in spite of occasional errors on the part of my client such as you are aware of."

"Well, if he won't co-operate, and she has no evidence, there doesn't seem to be much sense in serving papers," I remarked.

"Quite true, Major. Unfortunately, some counsel feel that the question of their prospective fees is paramount, and they are inclined to regard issues such as evidence, morality, and the best interest of the parties concerned as of secondary importance. And now, if you will excuse me. . . ."

I got up, picked my hat off the floor, and shook hands with him casually. His right was steady but weak, and the brittle skin dark blue with veins. He did not trouble to show me the door.

"If anything should come up, I'm at Arizona four-one-one-nine nine," I told him. "That will be confidential, if you don't mind. By the way, who does represent Mrs. Havers?"

He frowned upon me, ever so slightly, and mentioned a name, mouthing the syllables gingerly like slices of persimmon.

"Where's she living now?"

He improved on his frown and shook his head, no.

Outside, I strolled down the hallway and across the anteroom with my jauntiest air. The old girl behind the reception desk did a startled double take on me, but the elevator sucked me in before she could make up her mind to anything. I wondered if she figured maybe I ought to see a doctor.

Outside I communed some more with my pal the telephone directory, encased myself in a lonely booth, and dialed a Trinity number.

"Good after*noon!*" said a shrilly emphatic young lady. "This is Mr. *Insinger's* office, may I *help* you?"

"Sorry to trouble you," I said pleasantly. "McCann's Bookstore here. We've had a book on order for Mrs. Wilton F. Havers for sometime. It came in this morning, but we hear she's staying in Pasadena just now, and we were referred to you for her address."

"Oh, I *see.* Yes, sir, we *have it,* but I don't *think* we're supposed to *tell.* If you'd deliver the book to *us* . . ."

"Now, miss, be reasonable! We know Mrs. Havers is anxious to have it as soon as possible. She's not hiding or anything, is she, not from us surely? If you'll connect me with Mr. Insinger, perhaps . . ."

"I'm sorry, he's in *court.* Just a moment please."

She went into consultation with other members of the hired help. I could hear them buzzing among each other and an occasional fragment like, "Yes, but . . ." and "Oh, well . . ." After a spell of this she came back on the wire and said, "Sorry to keep you *waiting,* sir. Mrs. *Alice* Havers' address is six-oh-six-five Paxton *Road,* in *Flint*ridge."

I passed her a vote of thanks, jiggled the hook, and dialed Information for the number. My luck was as good as a silver penny that afternoon, the way I found all the right people in and all the wrong ones out. It saved a lot of time and patience. The information operator obliged, wanted some nickels in the slot, put me through, and there she was all right, on the button, with that special unmistakable coo in her voice that women affect when they expect a call from somebody they feel would want to be cooed at.

"Hellooh . . ."

"Good after*noon!*" I wished her in my best falsetto. "This is Mr. *Insinger's* office. Is Mrs. *Alice* Havers there, please?"

"Yes, this is she." Disappointed, that was she. I nursed my lips to keep from grinning.

"We had a *gentleman* here, Mrs. Havers, a Mr. *Micklejohn,* and Mr. *Insinger* has asked him to *call* on you. It's something about *evidence.* He's on his way out *now.*"

"All right, then," she said. "I'll see him. Thank you for calling."

We hung up on each other, and I walked out into the busy, sun-drenched street with my hat pushed back for better ventilation. The parking lot attendant had a map and showed me. Humming out on Figueroa, the old Packard seemed glad to shake the city dust and smoke.

I picked up Chevy Chase Drive at the Glendale intersection and drove leisurely north on its sinuous twists and hairpin bends through the Verdugo foothills. I'm not really much of a hand at kidding myself, but I figured it was up to me to start digging somewhere if we were ever going to have a hole made in this odd business.

Paxton Road corkscrewed for only three blocks or so from Highland Drive uphill, and lost interest there in a whitewashed barricade. I juggled the car around and backed it into the narrow driveway of a small English gray brick villa, crossed the lawn, and applied the front door knocker. A tiny, solidly barred judas opened almost instantly and gave a pair of skeptical pastel-green eyes a chance of looking me over. Lorna Mae's eyes, only a little harder, older, more critical, less speculative.

"Mrs. Havers? I'm Micklejohn. Mr. Insinger wanted me to . . ."

The door swung open and admitted me to a living room that would have been a source of pride and comfort to your average small tradesman or office clerk. For the rightful mistress of El Rancho Primavera, it struck me as being something of a letdown.

"They phoned me to announce you," she said, sizing me up. "It was a bit short notice. They didn't explain . . ."

"Mr. Insinger has engaged me to assist him in the development of the evidence in your case," I returned smoothly. "He has probably mentioned to you that certain angles should be more firmly established, if possible. Before I go to work on them, I thought it better to ask you a few questions."

"Oh, a private detective," she diagnosed, mildly interested. She came out of the front-door shadows, a tall, graceful, handsome brunette, forty-odd and not worried about it—good skin, no soft spots or wrinkles or surplus pounds anywhere. The hostess gown she could afford to wear with an air, an emerald silk job designed and cut by somebody unconcerned about the number of figures on a price tag. "Won't you sit down? Do I understand you already know all about my case then?"

"Not as much as I'd like, Mrs. Havers. Mr. Insinger tells me your husband means to put up a fight. Of course, under California law it's not necessary to prove anything drastic such as adultery, but even cruelty charges do after all have to be backed up by something substantial, if they're denied in court."

"Yes, we . . . I realize that," she said eagerly. "There's been a new development since yesterday that makes all the difference. We have witnesses now, good ones."

"Splendid," I said warmly, disciplining my tongue before it showed itself licking my chops. "About these witnesses," I prompted her. "What can they deliver?"

"Oh, it should do all right, I guess. My fine-feathered husband got tight last night and made a hard pass at a woman. She's the wife of some stupid ex-army officer, a guest at the ranch, and he got her out into the garden with him. That's enough evidence for mental cruelty, you know that. She'll have to testify, naturally— besides, they were observed."

"Hmm," I said, meaning just that.

It was too good to last, of course. The gods will let you get away with just so much before they catch up with you.

There was a swish of tires on the road and the tiny squeal of brakes. I had a quick peek through the open window at the plain black sedan with the buggy whip antenna and the two plain citizens climbing out of it. The smile froze around my lips so stiffly that it almost interfered with speech.

"Excuse me, Mrs. Havers. I'll have a drink of water in the kitchen, if you don't mind."

"Let me get it for you," she offered innocently. She wasn't such a bad scout. She just thought she knew all the answers. I made the kitchen door with several yards to spare, closed it behind me in her face and ducked out through the back door. They were already in the house and off their guard when I slipped in behind the wheel to coast silently out of the driveway.

"Hey! Hey, you!"

The motor caught in gear with an explosive roar and pulled me down the Paxton corkscrew at a merry clip. I hit Highland Drive, without bothering about the boulevard stop, going fifty in a cloud of dust. The Chevy Chase intersection came in sight before the first distant siren shriek found my eardrums. I had the jump on that radio car, not enough to make sure they couldn't have caught a glimpse of me on the highway junction but sufficient to fool them on the curves. Chevy Chase has more curves and less visibility to the mile than a Floradora chorus.

The country club driveway was a short, modest one, with a nice-sized parking lot full of shiny big cars. I slammed the brakes on, fifty yards away, and turned sedately, sliding in to park at the far end of the file. The siren screamed by on the highway, just as my feet touched asphalt. There wasn't even an attendant in sight to worry about it.

My watch said five-thirty, and the sun was already beginning to count the day's receipts. I walked into the clubhouse, found a comfortable chair in an inconspicuous corner, and struck a pose of weary boredom, always a cinch to keep the inquisitive and the sociable ones out of your hair. It seemed best to allow for a bit of time and frustration to take the sting out of the competition's excitement. Besides, I was by now commencing not to feel so good. I'm just a simple, ordinary, blue-eyed country boy, trying to make a living. I can be baffled with the rest of them.

The thing that had me stumped worst was where I couldn't for peanuts decide if this Alice in Wonderland business signified no more than crazy coincidence, or if I had been sitting on the brink of startling revelations when the competition came plodding in. And now there wasn't even a monkey's chance left to pick up the lead, if there was one. Now she'd know for sure I was a phony, even if I could get back at her somehow.

It had to be accidental. There were two separate matters, a wife tired of her husband's ways, anxious to have a divorce—a daughter kidnaped for ransom in mobster style. Water and oil don't mix. Mothers have admittedly been known to spirit children away with the idea of custody in mind, but they don't leave cryptic little notes about money or else. My Alice wouldn't believe in such tactics. She wasn't the type.

Not that the money wouldn't come in handy.

There was nothing in that, though. Havers, Sr., had all the money in California. If Alice went ahead and crammed a divorce down his throat, she'd soak him for a lot more than a quarter of a million, and she seemed to think she could do it. I wouldn't have been surprised. Those California judges will cut off the ball and chain if you can prove the party of the second part reads the paper at breakfast.

She had another guy on the waiting list, obviously, and what of it? It could be Luis Marescu, for all I cared. That might explain how she knew all about her "fine-feathered" husband playing Casanova by the swimming pool last night. Marescu's bungalow wasn't so far away. He might have been taking a stroll and "observing" the goings-on. He'd have hurried back to his telephone when the fun was over and told her all about it, chortling in his beard, it'd be such a break for them. She'd have her divorce, signed, sealed, and delivered, complete with a whopping big settlement; they could get married or something, and she'd have the stuff to invest in his precious colored movies. The money angle again. . . .

It still didn't make any sense.

It was a bit after seven and almost night when I climbed behind the wheel again. I felt reasonably certain that the heat would be off by then, but I took the long way home through Glendale, Burbank, and North Hollywood, coming down by Laurel Canyon to avoid the popular Cahuenga Pass where they like to check up on people. I didn't think they'd had a good look at the Packard, much less at the license plate, but our Fitzroy Drive building had a basement garage for its tenants, so I put the car to bed in its darkest corner before trotting up to the apartment.

From the kitchen a hot, spicy aroma of frying chicken drifted into my nose. The female of the Marshall species was curled up in her best pajamas with a magazine on the divan, perfectly composed and unperturbed. Women are odd creatures, operating on the strength of weird philosophies. She did not speak a word; she just smiled at me and held up her lipts to be kissed. I obliged and pitched my hat into a corner, dropping into the nearest chair.

"Henry call?" I inquired briefly.

"No, darling. Nothing happened at all. Did you have any luck?"

I grinned and showed her Spencer's penmanship on his check and card.

"Whee! Johnny, aren't you smart! Do you know, though, all afternoon I've been sitting here thinking how mean and selfish we really are, worrying only about our own predicament instead of trying to help that poor girl."

"Yeah, I know. We'll try, sugar plum. It'll work out O.K."

I wasn't so sure either. There was a very uncomfortable hunch kicking around in my tired brains that something was horribly fantastically wrong. This game of find the lady had a sinister joke in it somewhere.

And I wondered why Lorna Mae had wanted me to like her, what she'd had on her mind last night in the garden pergola when she called me a stupid idiot. Maybe I was one.

CHAPTER 5

THE PHONE woke us up at seven-thirty Wednesday morning. It was Henry all right, not quite so hearty as usual. He started talking fast as soon as I lifted the receiver.

"That you, Major? Things are breaking here. We had a special delivery letter half an hour ago. Mailed in Hollywood last night. Stiff cheap manila envelope, reinforced with cardboard— they enclosed her wrist watch; it's rather a good one, and I suppose they wanted to protect it in the mails. Enclosed a lock of hair, too. Hers all right, you've seen it, heavy red chestnut, easy to recognize. The note itself was exactly like the one they left behind in her bedroom, newsprint scissored out and pasted on a piece of our stationery. I copied it, like this: 'Havers, pack dough in plain suitcase, messenger service will call Wednesday morning, make sure no cops or else.' We're going to comply with the instructions in good faith; we're not even telling the Sheriff until tonight, unless she's back sooner."

"Nice!" I said. "This is a nice case, full of nice, considerate people. You're nice, the Sheriff's nice, the Boss is nice, hell, even the snatchers are nice, writing polite little notes and fixing it so her watch won't break. The only stinker in the whole game seems to be me. I'm the stubborn disagreeable son of a bitch who wants to spoil everybody else's fun. Well, O.K., we'll see."

"After all, what do you care?" he wanted to know. "It's not your money, and your name ought to be cleared soon."

"Uh-huh. Say, listen, something else. Did Havers ever get around to telling his wife about this?"

He paused for that one, long enough to show he didn't think much of it, but he bought it anyway.

"Why, yes, I believe he did. He mentioned talking to her yesterday, wanted her to meet him, but she wouldn't. So he explained over the phone."

"What time was that?" I asked nonchalantly.

"I'm sure I don't know, Major. Sometime in the afternoon, I expect. I don't like to pry into that situation very much. After all . . ."

"Yeah, and what's it to me," I said. "Forget it. Call me when there's more of this, will you?"

That he would, and please, I was to lay off. I hung up on him and rushed back into the bedroom, grabbing at my clothes. The little woman was already nearly respectable. She can be co-operative when she wants to. She listened to my story with the powder puff poised over her pretty nose.

"Johnny, what can we do? He's not altogether unjustified, is he? If we interfere, it might be dangerous for her. They might even kill her, you never know."

"Not much, they won't," I said confidently, wrestling with my shoelaces. "Ransom kidnapers don't kill. They're businessmen, they want to make a sale. Technically speaking the snatch is a gas-chamber felony, but so long as they don't harm the victim, it's a matter of a few years in San Quentin if they're caught. Might even get out of it altogether, if Havers wants to duck the trial publicity, which'd be just like him. The minute they kill somebody, they'll have every cop in the U.S. on their necks, and they've as good as booked their tickets to the bad place. I figure to jump on them while they're not looking and deliver the goods, lock, stock, and barrel. That's what Spencer's paying us for."

"Yes, darling. But if something should go wrong. . . . Aren't you forgetting how we got mixed up in this? It's true, what Henry says, they'll release her today, and she'll clear us."

I gave her a stare loaded with pity and reproach.

"Look, honeybee. You don't believe that, do you? You're a clever girl who's been brought up on the facts of life. This job was pulled by a small crew of smart amateurs, probably a man and a woman, who deliberately framed us for it. They're not going to unframe us again by allowing Lonny to see them; they'd be jolly careful about that anyway—no kidnaper's begging to be identified by his victim in a police line-up or from pictures. Chances are the man walked in on her behind a big bath towel, and she's had that same towel tied over her face ever since, with cotton in her ears and the rest of her trussed up like a pheasant ready for the spit. No, Suze, Lonny won't clear us—she'll suspect us. Come on, we've got to get going. I know where to find breakfast."

There was a small drive-in chow counter on Sunset, not more than fifty yards from the mouth of Lucerne Canyon and across the boulevard. It offered a splendid observation point from which to watch traffic in and out of the canyon. We backed the Packard in at eight-thirty sharp, ordered coffee and toasted muffins, and settled ourselves in anticipation of events to come, feeling singularly like cats supervising a very large and dubious mousehole.

This part of Sunset doesn't have much traffic, and the canyon had none at all. Once or twice a car would pull into the chow counter lot for a hot dog, but we were their only solid customers. We made them very happy. We had more coffee, and cokes, and Danish rolls and stuff. They must have thought we were God's own gift to the trade.

By eleven or so I was just beginning to grow a trifle uneasy when a bright blue delivery motor tricycle came puttering down the boulevard with a freckle-faced boy in a natty dark-blue uniform on board. He slowed down, studied the canyon signpost, switched gears, and turned smartly into the canyon, showing us the back of his closed package boot where it said Mercury Messengers, Inc.

The trip took him only twenty minutes, they were so ready for him. We could hear the purr of his mount from way up the canyon, coming down. He looked smug and pleased with himself turning back east onto Sunset. The package boot was propped open to allow for the upper half of a big brute of a suitcase, one of those striped gray airplane affairs, with its lower half fitting smugly inside. There were no straps or anything, but it looked like a fairly safe transport proposition.

We had it easy, that part of it. He droned merrily along in front of us, like a shiny blue bug, for miles and miles; sometimes I could afford to give him as much as three hundred yards. He kept right on Sunset all the way through Beverly Hills, over the Strip, and into Hollywood. Here I had to close in on him, and still the lights at Cherokee almost trapped me, but he slowed down and jockeyed through the traffic in a skillful U-turn to squeeze into the curb in front of a barbershop.

I stopped in a red zone and hopped out, keeping one eye on him.

"Park it, cookie. Anywhere you can stay in sight. I'll be back."

She nodded nervously, and I ambled across the boulevard. The messenger boy had it out now and was lugging it into the barbershop. It was only a small shop, four figaros, a shine jockey, and a white-coated cuticle butcher loafing over a magazine. She glanced up at the messenger and pointed to a corner of the shop, under the hatrack, and he dragged it over there and dumped it. He came

swaggering out again, mounted his cycle, and buzzed off in a cloud of exhaust smoke.

I strolled leisurely down the block to where my charming and able partner had found a berth for the car, and leaned in through the window.

"Check Point," I said briefly. "Nobody here yet, I think. I'm gonna get a shave."

"Johnny, they'll spot you!"

"No better disguise than a shave, cookie."

There was that to consider, but I was determined in any case not to lose sight of the bundle. It could always be they might try and pull a fast one. The pay-off in any snatch or extortion racket is a tricky business. It is more than that: it's the very essence of the whole thing, the really risky part, the one and only chink in the criminal's armor. Contact must be made by him, physical contact, regardless of how many innocent middlemen he tries to hide behind.

The barber was a surly old Italian who didn't try to tell me or sell me; he just went ahead and shaved me. I needed a shave anyway. Nothing happened. There stood my bundle in the corner under the hatrack, fat and sassy as you please, a mere trifling two hundred and fifty thousand simoleons in fives, tens, twenties, readily negotiable for any quantity of Scotch whisky, blondes, and clipper trips to Buenos Aires or Sydney, N.S.W.

"I better have a haircut, too, and a manicure," I told the barber.

He nodded and snapped his fingers, and the cuticle butcher reluctantly dropped *Esquire* and came over, trundling her caddy load of bottles and tweezers. She tackled my nails with reasonable skill, squinting at them with inches to spare, she was so myopic. Her spotlessly starched coat had a very short skirt with lots of leg in sleazy beige lisle hose under it, but her shoes were pretty fair.

"Good-looking piece of airplane luggage you've got there," I said after a while, making polite conversation.

"I guess so," she said indifferently. "Not ours. Left by a customer." She had one of those flat high Midwestern accents that turn sharp and querulous at the drop of a hat, but she was a fast worker. The barber wasn't quite through with me when she finished.

"It's my lunch hour," she told me significantly, straightening her skirt.

I slipped her a buck and a grin she wasn't having any of, and she put her things away, removed her coat, and trotted off to lunch in a thrifty little blue cretonne number. More customers came in and out, but not many, and none

interested in my suitcase. That was all right. Any damn fool could have peeked in from the busy sidewalk.

Time marched on. I bought a shoeshine as a last resort, and the colored boy was still working on me when an empty yellow cab pulled up outside, and the driver came bustling in.

"Package for Henderson here?" he inquired blithely of the assembled company.

Nobody seemed to mind. One of the barbers jerked a careless thumb at the hatrack corner. The driver wasted no words or gestures on it. He picked it up, hefted it appreciatively, and bustled right out again with it.

I made after him in a hurry on one dull and one gleaming shoe, having discovered a pressing appointment and dispensed suitable largess to appease the shine jockey's damaged pride of office. The cab made no trouble for us, though. It proceeded flag down in a leisurely fashion up Cherokee to Hollywood Boulevard, rolled east for a few blocks, and finished its journey in front of a snappy-looking restaurant near the Bronson intersection. Here the driver climbed out again and unloaded his freight, while we watched from less than fifty feet behind.

"Check point two," I said. "Your turn, glamorous. Should be the cloakroom. Go look-see, tactfully. I'll stay with the heap."

She came back soon after the empty cab had pushed off.

"Darling, you're so foxy. The cloakroom *does* have it. What'll I do, eat lunch? There's a snack bar near the entrance."

"That's the ticket. We could just sit here, they'll only send another cab or something, but since it's convenient you might as well hang on."

She nodded and clicked away again, swinging gracefully down the sidewalk with the sun striking a million sparks from the russet of her curls where they touched her eager young shoulders. I smiled and relaxed behind the wheel.

Time marched on some more. The boulevard traffic clanged, hooted, and shuffled by me in a long, remorseless stream. Several dull and innocent folks went in to patronize the restaurant, several others left it, having duly attended to stuffing themselves. A traffic cop came slowly put-putting on his motorcycle, marking tires of parked cars in this one-hour zone with his silly piece of chalk on a stick. He marked mine, casually glaring at me as he passed by. I was too smug and comfortable to sneer back at him.

Suzy came out at last, and my first glimpse of her made me snap out of it quick. She looked upset, and she was running. I hit the starter button, clashed gears, and threw the off-side door open, all in one motion.

"Johnny, it's gone!"

I swore unmusically, kicking myself in the shins for a dolt and a slacker.

"How? Were you asleep?"

"Of course not. I had an accident. One of those high stools at that snack bar, and some people pushed past me, and a woman stumbled and fell against me, so I fell off, and there was a lot of confusion and broken dishes, and when I looked it wasn't there anymore! And my legs hurt, and my hose are simply *ruined!*"

"Didn't you ask?"

"Yes, I did, and I was scared, too, but they just said it'd been collected."

"The service entrance!" I stormed, slipping the clutch with a loud bang and slicing away from the curb.

We tore around the next corner, defying the lights, in a frantic search for the inevitable service entrance alley, and got the shock of our lives. There was the alley, all right, and there was a car just coming out of it, if you want to call a ratty old 1929 Ford phaeton a car. There was the bundle, propped up conspicuously on the open back seat, looking perfectly insolent and altogether out of character, a huge expensive gray airplane suitcase riding in a rusty, battered jalopy. There was the driver, a cocky young lad in brown overalls and a wispy black mustache, pulling up and waving me on, blandly presenting me with the right of way.

It wasn't as if we had any option in the matter. I took my foot from the brakes and let the Packard roll by. My rearview mirror said he cut in behind me, and in the next block he passed me without showing the slightest concern.

"Honey, such *luck!*"

"Yeah, luck. I don't get it. I don't think I like this game any more. Too many wild deuces up people's sleeves. On the other hand, this could be the guy who doesn't know us. Or just another messenger boy. Soon find out."

He went right on making life simple for me. He turned west on Adams for a block or two, then south on Berendo—there were some dead and neglected palm trees on Berendo and a row of hopelessly ugly bachelor-apartment boxes, ancient yellow-brick firetraps that hadn't seen a painter's brush or a plumber's tool for years. They all looked exactly alike to me, but this kid was smart, he knew they were different. The right one he picked out, never hesitating, stopped in front of it, and proceeded calmly to unload my suitcase.

"This," I said sententiously, "would be just about it, if you ask me. The end of the line, and if it isn't, I'll know the reason why." I started to get out of the Packard, but the little woman caught my arm.

"But, Johnny, suppose they're waiting for us! If you think she's here, let's call the police!"

"Relax sugarplum. You sit here and take it easy. I've been waited for before. This ought to be a push-over."

We argued about it for a spell, while the kid dragged the bundle out of his buggy and started hauling it into the building. There wasn't another soul in sight, up or down the street. He was having a job with it, using both arms for a few steps at a time, stopping to change his grip, making another yard or two, stopping again to wipe the sweat. It was a hot day.

"Need a hand, fella?"

He looked up at me gratefully, his sallow young pinched face blank of recognition.

"Thanks, mister. Sure do."

I picked it up. I didn't think it was so heavy. Good old Superman Marshall.

"Just show me the way, fella."

He popped eyes and ran to open the basement door for me. It was a long, low, dark basement, littered with junk and smelly garbage cans. We walked right on through to the back, where he had another door to open with a key. This door had a room of sorts behind it, with a barred backyard window. It was furnished after a fashion, by a day bed, a table, a few chairs, and the usual bric-a-brac, all of it in various stages of disrepair but fairly clean.

"If you'll put it in the corner, mister, I can send it up later in the dumb-waiter."

I saw the service elevator panel, nodded, and did his bidding. This, I considered, was getting better and better all the time.

"You the janitor here?" I asked him, perching myself on one arm of his only so-called easy chair.

He nodded, yes, he was the janitor, but he didn't look grateful or happy any more. Somehow I had suddenly ceased inspiring confidence and good will in him. He wasn't cocky about it either; I had him plain worried, the way I sat there on the arm of his best chair, lighting a cigarette and forgetting to offer him one.

"Belongs to a tenant here, does it?" I suggested caustically, jerking my head at it.'

"What's it to you, mister? What you want?"

"Don't ask me, punk. Tell me. Who sent you to fetch it? Where are they now? When do you expect 'em back?"

He heard the rasp in my voice, and he'd lost what little complexion he had in the first place, but he was as game as they come. He got set with his bony little fists, called me a name that would have shocked an Algerian stevedore, and instructed me to withdraw presto and without delay.

"Tchk, tchk, such manners," I criticized, offering him a nasty grin. "Look, sonny, you want to

be more careful, you do for a fact. People might get cross with you when you talk like that. About that trunk now, huh? You gonna spill or do I push you around first?"

He swung on me, feinting with guttersnipe cunning, aiming for a foul, so I grabbed a handful of his jeans and braced myself and threw him ten feet or so against the wall. He bounced right back off it and flew at me, snarling. It almost seemed like a shame to hurt him, but I was good and irked by then. I stopped him with one in the stomach and cuffed his ears with a couple. He missed his footing, sprawled on the rug, and stayed there, sobbing his heart out, not unduly damaged, just scared and frustrated and mad at me.

"Oh, Lord and butter," I said wearily. "Will you behave, forchrissake, you little so-and-so, and make some sense? I haven't got time for you to throw fits in. Come on, now, you're O.K.; get up from there and we'll talk it over. Might be a couple of bucks in this for you."

But no, it was no use. He stayed right where he was, biting the rug and crying fit to kill. All I could do was sit and smoke my cigarette and wait for him to come out of it. I'm not so much of a hand at hurting them when they're down. The whole thing struck a sour and embarrassing note, and

I found myself wishing the little woman had come along, She'd have known how to handle this. I had half a mind to go and bring her in.

The balloon went up before I got anywhere. They must have had lots of experience walking on tiptoes and opening doors quietly, because my hearing was in excellent shape and just the same they had me foolishly peering straight down the barrels of their .38 Police Specials before I had a chance to so much as flick an eyebrow. It was my old pals Mike and Ike of the Colchester Arms, regarding me with a good deal of disapproval and with an obvious lack of fond affection.

"O.K., bub, reach!" Mike recommended discourteously.

I looked back at him without pleasure and without moving more than strictly necessary to take the cigarette from my lips, blow a thin streamer of smoke and replace the cigarette. I was very unhappy and wanted urgently to bounce a couple off my own nose, but I didn't need him to help me.

A small dark Mexican girl with very wide, frightened eyes burst past Ike through the kitchen door and flung herself upon the janitor kid, wailing and yammering at him in a torrent of tearfully passionate Spanish. The drift of it seemed to be that she had heard us from the kitchen, and *instantemente* she had known I was a pretty *malo hombre,* so when the argument started she had run out into the yard and rushed to the coin-box phone in the lobby upstairs, and the *telefonista* had promised to send help, and here it was, so everything was jake now, and she loved him very much. It was quite pathetic, all the way round. I felt pathetic myself. The kitchen had never even occurred to me. The operator would have signaled a holdup to county headquarters, they'd have radioed the nearest detective prowl car, and here we were, just as she said, one big happy family.

Mike didn't think so. He was annoyed with me. I was supposed to reach, and I wasn't reaching or anything. He shuffled his feet to a more convenient stance, drew a bead on the pit of my stomach, and repeated his advice. We were still looking at each other, and I was still allergic to him. I blew some more smoke and shook my head.

"Whaddayaknow!" said Ike. "We got a hard boy!"

"Yeah," Mike said, scowling thoughtfully. "I seen him before, but I don't mug him. Who did you say you was, bub?"

I thought that was reasonably funny, so I laughed at him. Nothing hilarious, a mere polite tinkle. He didn't appreciate that.

"Aw, nuts," he reproved me. "O.K., so it's a pinch."

Ike came up behind me on cat

feet, dug his gun into my kidneys, and explored with one hand for artillery emplacements. "Clean," he admitted, obviously disappointed.

"Uh-huh," said Mike, grudgingly. "O.K., let's go, bub. Hey, mister, you better come along, swear out a heist beef."

The janitor kid was sitting on the day bed by then, with his Mexican doxy beside him, wiping his face with a smudgy handkerchief and crooning over him. He stared at us dumbly and nodded without a great deal of enthusiasm. The girl promptly got excited again and spat another stream of Spanish at us. Sure, her Carlos, he would come and swear out the *acusación,* just as soon as he felt better. She'd bring him herself, in his own car. They shrugged at her and scowled some more. Aw nuts, O.K. Did she know where the station was? Oh, yes, she did. The station. *Si, señor!*

It was a lovely mess and no mistake. I had no choice, of course. I knew they wouldn't listen to reason, but I couldn't afford to walk out of there with them and leave the bundle in the joint.

"That suitcase in the corner, gents," I said diffidently. "Be a good idea to get a load of what's in it, and then I'll tell you an interesting story."

"Suitcase, huh, bub?" grunted Mike, suspiciously.

He jerked his head. Ike stepped right up, snapped the locks and gadgets on it, and threw it open. I'll say this for him, he didn't faint or even jump much higher than two feet and a few inches. I could have taken the pair of them then. For ten seconds or so they were dizzy. I could have swung at them from way back here and laid them out ever so pretty. The way it turned out, it's an awful pity I didn't.

"Holy suffering cats!" said Mike at last, when he found his breath serving his groggy larynx again. He did not say it angrily, or with much reverence to it either. He was just plain surprised out of his limited supply of wits.

"Yeah," I said. "Whaddaya-know. Ain't *that* something? O.K. Now will you listen to me, Kennedy?"

Not much, he would. A crafty leer pulled at the corners of his round sweaty face. His gun arm came up again, stiffly. He had my number now. He was hep to me. I couldn't tell *him* anything.

"So it's you, bub," he said grimly. "Now that's real nice, huh? Now we're getting somewhere. They took some swell pitchers of you and the broad, bub. At the depot, see? That's how come I didn't mug you before, without the broad. She wouldn't be around here, would she?"

"No, bub," I said, feeling exasperation knotting up to a hard sour ball in my stomach. "But

Miss Havers might be. In fact, I wouldn't be surprised if she's upstairs in one of the apartments. Ask the punk, he ought to know."

"Frisk the joint," he told his stooge, waving me back into my chair with the gun.

Ike was goggling at me. The facts were still slippery to the groping butterfingers of his mind. He knew it was me, but the rest of it was almost too difficult to cope with.

"Hey, sarn't, you figure he'd—"

"Go on!" Mike said stonily. "Frisk the joint."

After a while Ike came back alone, perspiring profusely, his round, rough baby face more blank than before. He threw the passkey on the table, holstered his gun, and produced a pair of clinking bracelets.

"Sorry, gents," I said. "Nothing doing."

Mike sized me up in one speculating glare.

"You wouldn't want us to flop you, now would ya, bub?" he inquired.

"You can try, if you like," I told him quietly. "It has been done. On the other hand, you can take me along easy and not bother with the nippers. It's up to you, Kennedy. I'm not resisting arrest, not unless you make me."

"Aw, nuts," he said, scintillating as always. "O.K., pick up the grip an' let's go."

Ike drove north on Berendo up to Pico Boulevard and turned west, while I pondered uncomfortably over the errors of my ways and the tricky hand that Fate had seen fit to deal me. Life, I knew, was going to be both real and exceedingly earnest. They might fail to make any sort of rap stick to us, but as the cards were stacked now, they'd certainly do their damnedest. We might actually have to stand trial, as I saw it, and spend every penny we owned. If our luck held out on us like this, we might even run the risk of conviction.

This was about the point I had reached when Ike turned off Pico into San Vicente, which was fundamentally a very sound move on his part, because San Vicente happens to be quite a convenient short cut. We had been rolling on it in splendid isolation for perhaps half a mile when my eyes roved to the driving mirror and blinked. The blunt radiator nose of a Packard showed in the mirror, rapidly closing in behind us.

It happened so fast I still have trouble trying to recollect events in the right sequence. The Packard overtook us in a burst of speed, sending a whoof of displaced air and exhaust gas through our open windows. It sliced brazenly across the road in front of us, with a stark scream of brakes that jarred my bones clear down to the ankles. Ike yelped like a dog with its tail caught in the front door. He stamped on his own pedals desperately and twisted the Chrysler toward the railroad embankment on our right.

Mike never had a chance to make a noise. My left traveled in a vicious hook and smashed into his throat, my right had a claw grip on the cylinder of the gun on his knees. His trigger finger worried for an impotent second before he released the gun and sagged against me. I shoved him aside and gave Ike the butt behind his right ear, the moment he succeeded in holding the Chrysler with one wheel on the embankment slope and one nudging the Packard's running board. The whole affair had that eerie, spectacular neatness touch of a very bad dream or of the prize stunt of a very clever stage magician.

Suzy came running to jerk the door on my side open. She was swinging a jack handle and looking like the original wild woman from Borneo, gray eyes wide and flashing, hair flying all over her face, chin stuck out in furious determination. I laughed at her and climbed out.

"All set, luscious. Here we go again. The boys won't mind, they're asleep."

I had to be kissed with a good deal of abandon before she'd let me push her back into the Packard and shove off. One or two cars and a train went by during all this, in both directions, but nobody seemed sufficiently intrigued to stop and inquire. In this part of the world they've seen too many movies being shot.

"Darling, I was *so* scared! I saw them arrive and sneak after you into that dirty basement, and I nearly ran to phone the police, but I knew you wouldn't want me to. So finally, I decided to park in an alley and come back to help you, and then it was too late, they were coming out with you between them, and those guns! Oh my gosh, Johnny, the *money!* You forgot—"

That was a laugh, that was. I explained, carefully and tactfully. It took her most of the way home to Westwood to grasp it all and be properly horrified.

"You don't think they'll make off with it, do you?" she wondered with a doubtful frown.

"No, cherry pie. They wouldn't know what to do with it. Listen, I've been wanting to ask you something. That woman who tripped you at the restaurant, what was she like?"

Her frown improved itself with concentration.

"I don't remember exactly," she said slowly. "She was a pale blonde, I believe, not very tall, too much make-up, a cheap blue dress, and thick ugly lisle hose. She apologized a lot, and she tried to help me, but she seemed awfully nervous and clumsy."

"Yeah," I said. "She would be."

CHAPTER 6

WE STAYED home and in generally low spirits for the rest of that Wednesday and for most of Thursday. Nothing happened to relieve the monotony or our uncomfortable apprehensions for more than twenty-four hours, except for the minor incident of the Wrong Number. This befell us on the Wednesday night, somewhere around nine, and at the time failed to register much of an impression on me, although I was to remember it and to realize its significance on a later occasion. Too much later.

But there really seemed nothing to it then. The phone rang, and I carelessly answered with the magic words, "Arizona four-one-one-nine-nine," mere force of cagy habit, since of course we were expecting Henry to call, and incidentally not looking forward to the pleasure with any great deal of eager anticipation, what with one thing and another.

However, the wire kept silence for a second or two, and then a female voice said, "Oh . . ." That was all, that and the click of disconnection and the empty dial tone hum.

Henry never did phone. He made a personal appearance on Thursday afternoon, a bit after five, knocking on our door and then walking in on us with his own key to the joint. He looked tired and nervous, and he didn't bawl us out at all, not even after I had lamely confessed to the whole dismal array of mistakes and dire events of that inauspicious Wednesday.

"I had an idea that was about how it happened," he admitted, having heard me out. "I meant to come down here before, but everything at the ranch has been in a constant uproar from the moment we received the bad news. You've simply no idea, Major. The Sheriff came and returned the money to us himself, around dinnertime, and he brought along those men of his who arrested you. They were furious, I can tell you. And the Boss hit the ceiling. I've never seen anything like it. There was another officer, a detective lieutenant from the Sheriff's headquarters, chap named Hogan or something; he and I spent hours trying to calm the others down. Sensible chap he was, never did get excited. Of course, they were all mad at each other. Mr. Havers at the Sheriff, because his men had interfered with the ransom payment, and the Sheriff at him, because he'd been kept in the dark, and both of them together at these men, because they let you escape."

"And the whole bunch of 'em at us, naturally," I prompted him.

"Well, you can't blame them," he reminded me naïvely.

"But Mr. Fl—Henry, I mean," said Suzy, "why did they imagine we left the money behind when we escaped? We had every opportunity—"

"They think you lost your nerve," he told her. "This Lieutenant Hogan did bring up the point, though. I was almost tempted to confide in him later on.

"Well, anyway, they've been conferring all night and most of today, and they've decided now to wait for new instructions from you," Henry said awkwardly. "The Sheriff finally promised co-operation, provided we'd keep him informed, and he won't interfere with another attempt at payment, but as soon as Lonny's released he plans to crack down on you. Of course, when she returns you'll be all right, really, because then she can—"

"Sure, sure. We can hardly wait," I said. "You just call us the minute these precious new instructions arrive. I have a hunch my bungling days are just about over."

"But, Major! My God, you're not going to interfere with that ransom again, are you? This has been bad enough as it was, but another go like that and they're sure to kill her, they're bound to feel we won't pay, we only want to catch them!"

"Now see here, Henry," I said crisply, "it's true we fouled it up pretty good yesterday, but we made a deal with you, brother, and we expect you to deliver, regardless. But you can take my tip

that the next time there aren't going to be any more slip-ups on this."

I had to admit to myself he took it well, even if he did wince once or twice. He sat and thought it over for a while, and at last he made up his mind.

"I'll stick to my end of our bargain, if you want me to. And that's not merely a blind vote of confidence. The more I think about this terrible case, the more I become personally convinced that you're right, that there's an inside connection somehow, and that it would be a mistake to pay ransom without making at least an effort to forestall these criminals. I've been worrying over what you said about Mr. Marescu," he continued. "You don't trust him, do you?"

"No, not particularly," I conceded. "Made some inquiries about him, though, and found out that at least he is what he claims to be."

"He left the ranch Tuesday after lunch," said Henry, significantly. "And he's disappeared, or so it seems!"

"You don't say. How'd you find that out?"

I wasn't much interested. It sounded like another silly coincidence or like a simple misunderstanding somewhere. But Henry was not to be denied.

"It was reasonable enough that he should want to go," he said, "though Mr. Havers asked him to stay. They got along fairly well together, and he'd been helpful in the morning—mostly by talking against you and all that. Then after he left, the servants found his shaving kit he'd forgotten to pack, and both Margaret and I have tried to call him about it several times yesterday and today at his place in Sherman Oaks. Each time we got the same answer from his butler: he hasn't come home yet. So that started me thinking, and then I began to remember things. You know the Boss was discussing his invention with him? I'm under the impression that we were going to turn him down, *and* that he was aware of it."

"Yeah? Well, hell, there are other millionaires besides Havers. I've heard even the banks will break down and make you a loan sometimes. What did he want to do it the hard way for? Besides, I've got some reason to think he had other expectations, and I've an idea where he might be found, too."

Henry stared at me, slightly nonplused.

"There's just this," he told me. "I called a friend of mine this afternoon, a woman with more than twenty years' experience in the field of Hollywood publicity, and asked her about him. She advised me in confidence that she's heard his invention isn't worth a penny —some of it old stuff, the rest im- practical and full of bugs. And she said he used to be heavily involved with the Lefkovitz group here in the early thirties. Labor racketeers, business extortion, if you remember. I know all that doesn't prove anything, but you'd hinted you weren't satisfied with him, and then there was an incident last week I didn't pay much attention to at the time, but it came back to me, and it does look peculiar now."

"Oh, an incident," I said intelligently, still pretty skeptical.

"It was Friday night," he explained eagerly. "I had taken a girl home from dinner and a movie, and driving back I lost my way in the hills about the Strip. It's dark up there and easy to miss a turning. I'm not even completely sure yet where I went wrong, but on the map I can probably figure it out."

He'd actually brought a map to show me. They have a lot of hills in that town, some of them pretty rugged, but people like to live in them, and the result is often a crooked maze of little dead-end serpentine streets clustering together in an almost hopeless tangle.

"This girl lives up here on Appian Way," he pointed out with a pencil. "So I took her up by Sunset Plaza Drive and came back the same way to here, I think. That's where Sunset Plaza has another sharp elbow, but I missed that and must have hit this one, that'd be Morningview Drive, which goes up again after a few hundred yards—so I realized then, and turned back, and almost ran into Marescu's car coming out of a road or a driveway, about here—must be a driveway, there's no road marked. I know it was his car, wine-red Pierce-Arrow, custom-built job, you can't mistake it. I kidded him about his driving at breakfast on Saturday, and he became very much annoyed and denied he'd been out at all that night. He went so far as to suggest I'd been drinking."

I slapped him on the back and gave him a drink and told him to forget it, I'd call him in the morning and slip him the office on Master Marescu's mysterious nocturnal excursions. He couldn't be persuaded, kept on telling me I was a fool trying to tackle a potential gang of racketeers by myself, but he gave up in the long run and finally left us, still shaking his head. We both agreed he was a real nice boy, but a shade too romantic.

CHAPTER 7

THE unincorporated community of Sherman Oaks straddles Ventura Boulevard between Studio City and Encino on the San Fernando Valley fringe. My old pal the telephone book met me at an all-night filling station on Ventura and gave me the address of Mr. Luis Marescu at 9516 Segovia Avenue.

We found it around 2:00 A.M. that screwy Thursday night, a modern "functional" concrete and glass-brick villa, on top of a small landscaped knoll some hundred yards aloof from the dark and empty street. I switched the Packard's lights to dim, and we sat looking at it and at each other for a minute, without much confidence or enthusiasm.

I've never had much affection for crossword puzzles, and I felt strongly that while we were about it, we might as well seek to learn about the fastidious Mr. Marescu's connections with it all, if any.

"Darling, do you think he'll be home now?" said Suzy, skeptically. "After all, if he's been gone for two days. . . ."

"Soon find out," I said. "Henry phoned to his butler, and butlers usually know a sight more than they tell over the phone."

"What made you hint to Henry that you had an idea where he might be?" she asked me. "And something about his expectations of investment money elsewhere?"

I smiled at her and told her the story of my Tuesday afternoon adventures in Flintridge, having spared her the account up till then to save her undue alarm and speculation. She was shocked and impressed, and instantly convinced that I must be right.

"Wouldn't that be just like him though! Playing both ends against the middle, making sure he'd get his hands on the Havers money, either from him or from her."

"Yeah, it's a cruel world," I said. "Only, you can see now that the guy doesn't make sense to figure in this snatch game. Just the same, I'm anxious to find out where he does figure. Come on, let's go."

We climbed up through the garden to the front door, and I leaned against the bell; we were getting a bit weary of breaking into places and suffering a bloody nose every time, so we thought we'd brazen this one out.

"Yes, sah? What you want?"

He was good and mad at us for getting him out of bed at that hour—a husky, broad-shouldered Filipino in striped silk pajamas, his big almond eyes blearily pugnacious.

"Mr. Marescu come in yet?" I asked him pleasantly.

It seemed like a simple and natural question to me, but he didn't think so. He took a full minute to consider, before he tried to slam the door in our faces. I got my foot in first and gave him some exercise for his efforts to push me out. We must have made a noise while we were abut this, because the moment I was in the hall and getting set to bust him one, the lights went

on, and there was our friend himself, looking annoyed and gesturing at us with a small black pistol.

"Here, Ricardo, what the devil! Oh, it's you, is it?"

He wasn't afraid of me, not with a gun in his hand. After the first second of surprise he was pretty smug about it, especially when he saw Suzy behind me. It did not even occur to him apparently that a hot couple of criminals as we were understood to be might prove uncomfortable to handle. Why, good evening, madame. Come right in, both of you. He was vain enough to push his permanent back in place and to arrange the collar of his expensive blue brocade kimono for us, with his left.

The living room was a symphony in chromium, six different bright shades of leather and two extra large Picasso daubs of matadors and prostitutes. The Filipino glared at us as we filed in, hesitated, and slunk away, muttering.

Our host knew exactly how these things were done. He'd been sitting in a canvas chair for all these many years, shouting instructions at a long succession of leading men with similar problems on hand. He held the little pistol just so, where the camera could pan on it good, he moved back across the room with the gracious self-assurance of a ballet dancer, he bestowed a handsomely photogenic warning smile upon us.

"Do sit down, if you wish," he invited us brightly. "They might be a few minutes." He'd backed up to the telephone taboret and was feeling for the receiver.

"Before you get too playful," I said, grinning at him, "let me tell you something, Jackson. You better learn about guns, if you're going to use one in your business."

"My dear man, I don't profess to understand why you came here or what you're talking about," he said sonorously, checking up on his hand with a quick glance. "But I'd advise you not to trifle with me, because I shall most certainly shoot you down like a dog in the attempt, and in front of the lady, if necessary."

"Relax," I said. "We're only here to ask you a couple of questions, not to play games with you. Just remember next time you think you've caught a crook not to hold your gun like that. This way you can't hit the side of a barn, and I could take your silly toy away from you before you tried."

He turned up one corner of his mouth, registering scorn, and reached for the phone again. He knew all about these situations. He'd show me. You can't take a man's gun away from him before he shoots you dead, and he could so hit the side of a barn.

I flipped my burning cigarette on the rug, a yard or two to his right, distracting his attention as per schedule, and took his gun away, with a swift grip on the recoil slide to block the firing pin. We both started laughing at him. He was much too astonished to make a squawk about it. He stared, bug-eyes, as if I'd suddenly turned into a boa constrictor. These things weren't being done this season.

"So now you know, Jackson," I said, stepping on the cigarette butt to kill it. "Don't fool around with those. Where were you last Friday night?"

We had him worried now, but not enough for that.

"I fail to see why that should concern you," he told me indignantly.

"Please, Mr. Marescu, you don't understand," Suzy persuasively intervened. "We didn't take Lonny Havers, and we don't believe you did, but we're trying to find her. We interviewed Mr. Fleming today, and he claims to have seen you out in your car that night. You almost hit him, coming down from a place in the hills north of Sunset. Is that true?"

By now he didn't know what to think any more, or it may have suited his book to pretend as much.

"I refuse to be intimidated!" he shouted at us. "There was a lady involved, and I don't propose to go into the matter any further! Fleming can open his irresponsible blabber mouth all he cares, it means nothing to me, do you understand? Nothing!"

"All right, chief, all right," I said soothingly, commencing to see some daylight. "Skip the lady, we're not interested in *that* one. Where was it you ran into Fleming—somewhere off Sunset Plaza?"

"Certainly not!" he countered, clearly surprised; it sure was his night of surprises. "If that's what he told you, he must have been drinking, as I suspected at the time." The anticlimax of it had sobered him to almost human speech.

"Johnny, let's leave him alone. You can see how it is, we can't make him tell the rest of it if he doesn't want to. Mr. Fleming made a mistake, that's all."

"Oh, yes, we could, if I thought it mattered." I jerked the magazine from his gun, snapped the cartridge out of the chamber, and was about to throw the lot into a handy wastepaper basket when the vaguest wisp of a whiff drifted lazily up into my nostrils.

I took a closer look and sniffed at the muzzle of the little .32 Mauser.

"Don't tell me I've been underestimating you, chief," I said. "This thing smells like it's been exercised since the last fourth of July!"

He didn't move a muscle or make a sound, he just kept on glaring. I shrugged, dropped his handful of old iron in the basket, and took the little woman's arm.

"So long, chief," I said over my shoulder from the door. "Give my regards to Alice, and tell her I'm sorry. For both of you."

The back-seat question didn't arise until we got back to Westwood around three-thirty that night, but when it came, it made up for lost time in a hurry, and with that quaint, irresistible touch of gruesome irony to it that life is always so ready to provide at the drop of a hat.

That was precisely what did it: the drop of a hat. What happened was that we drove into the basement garage of our building, parked in our usual dark corner behind a concrete pillar, and started to get out, both of us more than slightly weary, cross, and disillusioned with ourselves. At this point my right foot clumsily caught in the pedals, and in trying to straighten myself out I knocked my hat off and it fell behind me in the dark tonneau. This, naturally, caused me to refer without generosity or good will to both the hat and myself, and to reach down for it over the front seat's edge.

My groping fingers met a textile fabric they did not recognize as germane to either a hat or to the Packard's upholstery. It felt, however, strangely like a rough woolen sports jacket, with something bulky and yielding under it. I made a sound somewhere between "Arr!" and "Hey!" pulled my arm in very fast indeed, and fumbled for the dome light switch.

"What's wrong, Johnny?"

"Don't look now, pussycat," I said, none too steadily. "We have a back-seat passenger. He's asleep, I hope."

He was curled up in the tonneau with his legs on the seat and the rest of him on the floor, and with my hat covering his face, since he didn't have his own with him. I took my pencil flash out to help the domelight, shone the beam down on him, and reluctantly moved the hat. Bob Havers, grimacing up at me with wildly frightened eyes and a wide-open mouth brimming with imperfectly clotted, gory red blood.

Let it be recorded here to our credit that we didn't make a song and dance about it. We jumped out and stood looking at each other for a moment, breathing a trifle faster than usual, before we made a dash for the stairs to our apartment.

"That's torn it!" I said fervently, fitting my key into our front door lock. "This is where we came in. From now on this is strictly the Sheriff's baby! I'm gonna—Say, listen, did we leave the lights on in here when we went out?"

There was a thin strip of light showing under our doorstep. Suzy caught at my hand.

"I don't think so. . . ."

I pushed her aside, slipped Mike's .38 out of my pocket, and barged in through the door, instantly flattening myself against the wall and covering the man who sat peaceably reading a magazine in our best chair under a bridge lamp.

He merely glanced up at me and waved a languid gesture of welcome with his cozily drawing cigar.

"Morning, Major! You're out kinda late, aren't you? I'm Hogan, Sheriff's confidential squad, detective lieutenant. Sorry to bust in on you like this, but we were anxious to contact you soon's possible."

"Oh, were you?" I said. "How the devil did you get in here?"

"Manager's passkey," he told me briefly. "Would the Missus be with you, Major? You two have a little explaining to do."

"Let's see your ticket," I suggested, and he lifted the magazine from the open wallet on his lap. He'd had it waiting for me there all the time; he knew exactly how I'd feel coming in and finding him there. I grinned at him foolishly and tucked the gun back in my pocket. Suzy came in behind me, and he got up and bowed at her, he was so polite.

"O.K., Lieutenant," I said. "Maybe I was wrong and there is one halfway smart cop in this county after all. I'd like to know how you found us here, though. This joint's supposed to be our secret hide-out."

"Can't beat police routine," he said complacently. "Nobody can. We've had six cars out, these past three days and nights, checking all recent subleases in apartment buildings, just on the off chance. Boys would show your pictures to the managers and regular tenants. Somebody bound to notice you. Hell, man, we knew you were there, you could be found."

"That's fine," I said. "Just fine. So now, we're pinched. That suits me, brother. We've had a bellyful, both of us."

He almost smiled, but he didn't quite remember how to go about it.

"No pinch," he said dryly. "There are a couple of raps we could do you for, like dangerous driving, resisting an officer, damaging county property. We'll skip it, if you'll behave good. Which reminds me, Sergeant Kennedy'd like his gun back you borrowed."

I gave it to him, with a dazed, glassy stare to keep it company, and he glanced at it casually to see if I hadn't hurt it, and said: "You-'re not surprised, are you, Major?" as if that would have been altogether too silly of me.

"But look, Lieutenant," said Suzy in a very small voice. "We thought the Sheriff had made up his mind we were kidnapers and everything. . . ."

"Well, you did your best to make it up for him," he pointed out. "Fact is, I want to ask you a few simple questions about that. But we know you didn't snatch the Havers girl. Checked your prints with Washington, got our answer this afternoon. Found the cabby who took you from Lucerne Canyon to your hotel, Monday night. Checked back your movements last Wednesday, when the pay-off went blooey. No, we know you're in the clear. Course it stands to reason, we want to hear from you what you been up to, why you ducked out of the ranch that night, what all you know about this thing. You folks have been kinda hard on our nerves, bumming around on your own like that."

"Go on with you," I said cynically. "You know damn well we had no choice in the matter. Havers has your boss jumping through hoops for him. You were no more interested in grabbing the snatchers than in catching pneumonia, not before the bundle changed hands, once Havers said to lay off. Any sheriff fitted with standard intestinal organs would have gone right ahead regardless and called in the F.B.I., too. And you expect us to sit by and watch our characters get mucked up, maybe spend a few weeks in the can on my terminal leave?"

"Well, now, Major, as to that I couldn't say. Mr. Havers is kind of an important man around these parts, and it stands to reason he'd get excited about a thing like this and maybe try shoving us a bit. It would be up to him to have the Federal boys in on it, and even then they won't usually do much for thirty days, unless you can show there's a chance of your party having crossed a state line. You don't think she has, do you?" he added significantly.

I blinked at him, pretty much startled and gratified.

"I take it all back," I told him. "You've actually doped this one out, you have. No, Lieutenant, I don't think our little Miss Muffet would cross any state lines. She didn't need to."

"So you do know," he said calmly.

"Yeah, and I've been kicking myself in the pants ever since," I confessed, making rueful faces, "for letting her get away with it, playing me for the world's champion heavyweight sucker."

"Darling, whatever are you talking about?" Suzy inquired, completely bewildered.

"I haven't dared tell you yet," I said. "Because I couldn't be sure, and anyway I don't enjoy looking like a goon any better than the next guy. Lieutenant Hogan and I both think Lonny kidnaped herself, that's all."

"Johnny, no! How could she? Whatever for?"

"It goes like this," I told her un-comfortably. "Lonny's fond of her mother and decided she was getting a raw deal—probably heard her father say he'd let her starve before he'd give her a divorce, or words to that effect. She probably went downtown sometime last week, rented an apartment in that dump on Berendo, and got herself a job as a manicurist in the barbershop on Sunset. On Monday night she was all set with her plans, but she felt uneasy about them, and if I'd only been a bit more kindly disposed to her when she took me out in the garden, chances are she'd have confided in me. But I had to growl at her, and she got her dander up and went right ahead with it, running away in the Cadillac, leaving a note, and next day mailing her own watch and a lock of her hair with the pay-off instructions.

"There was nothing much to it, so long as her father played ball, as she figured he would. Chances were she could just send a messenger to collect, take the stuff to a safe deposit, and leave it there until Mamma might need some ready cash in her business. Then she could go back to the ranch in a day or two, dish up some kind of a yarn about her adventures, and be everybody's brave little heroine."

"The manicurist!" said Suzy, still very much puzzled. "But she did your nails, you talked with her, and you didn't know her!"

"Huh, I even tipped her a buck for the job! What about you, she tripped you in the restaurant and apologized to you and helped you not to notice her apartment janitor collecting the bundle from the cloakroom, right under *your* nose! She's a reckless, stubborn, crazy high-school kid of seventeen, who's been reading too many stories about gangsters and gun molls. She bleached her hair, she bought glasses and cheap clothes, she practiced a Kansas City accent. I took one hell of a good look at her in the shop, but not from *that* angle. . . . Still, I'd have nabbed her easy, later on, if that dumb Mexican janitor hadn't crossed me up. He was sweet on her, of course. There's only one thing that has me worried, on account of it doesn't fit so good. My cigar butt."

"You got a point there, Major," said Hogan, his marble blue eyes inscrutable.

"Darling, if you offended her that night. . . ."

"Yeah, but not that much," I said. "How could she know we were going to run off as we did?"

"Which reminds me," Hogan said. "Why did you?"

I explained, and he scratched his gray chin thoughtfully.

"Mr. Havers should have mentioned that to us," he commented, sadly shaking his head. "The way folks cooperate with us on their own troubles, and still expect us to dig them out. . . ."

"You did tell me her mother didn't seem much worried," Suzy said. "But what a horrid creature she must be, allowing her own daughter to do a thing like that!"

"I'm not satisfied she knew," I countered. "But I'll bet our friend here is."

"Sure," said Hogan, imperturbably. "I saw Mrs. Havers before coming up here. She was worried all right, but not so much as she'd be if there was a mob involved. She told me the kid had suggested the idea to her weeks ago, a few days after she left her husband, but naturally she took it for just a joke, or anyway nothing worse than a silly girlish whim. She also told me about your visit, Major."

"You don't say. I should think you knew all about that on Tuesday."

"I slip one every now and then," he admitted reasonably. "That was me you ran away from Tuesday. I came up with a deputy from our Pasadena Substation to get a routine statement, and finding you there never occurred to us. We thought you were just another fancy boy with a fast line in con stuff or something. Chased you clear down to Figueroa, and then we got a call on the Havers Cadillac having been found abandoned in Hollywood, and I never did have time for another go at the old lady until last night. Then, when I showed her your picture—"

"Lieutenant, are you certain she isn't hiding the child right now?" Suzy interrupted with a frown. "I understand how Lonny must have felt when she discovered what had happened to the money, Wednesday afternoon—she'd hear from the janitor, of course, and she'd have to give up both the apartment and the job instantly, knowing the police would be checking back. And yet she couldn't go home, either, not to her father, for how could she explain herself?"

"She's going to try again," I said confidently. "She'd never run for cover behind Mamma's skirts. That is a very stubborn young woman, and she's convinced she's smarter than all the rest of us put together. We'll fix her on the next take."

"Which reminds me," Hogan said again, level-eyed. "You seem to have been awful busy on this, Major, digging way deep down. How come?"

I grinned at him and showed him Spencer's card, and the check I hadn't cashed yet. He almost buried his nose in them, moving his lips as he spelled out every word in a whisper, ". . . investigate Miss L. M. Havers' kidnaping and all related matters. . . ." Otherwise he kept his face perfectly straight and unastonished.

"I'll see to it that you get cleared with Mr. Havers," Hogan said, "But we'll expect you to leave po-lice matters to us. From now on, the only place for both of you in this is the back seat—"

He stiffened at the sound of our chorus of groans. They must have been very genuine, harrowing ones. We'd almost completely forgotten about Bob.

CHAPTER 8

"IN THE NECK," said the doctor flatly.

He was a very tall, awkward looking oldster, a sloppy dresser with a rough, abrupt manner, but his big hands moved with a quick deftness, smoothly skillful as if they were well-paid independent associates, accustomed to frequent much better social circles and a little contemptuous of the boss.

We all stared at him in silence, the whole crowd of us, as he bent to his task. They had pushed some tenants' cars out to make more room, and brought in portable floodlights, cameras, and all manner of stuff. A mortician's ambulance was backed up with its receiving end to the garage entrance.

The grisly remains of Robert Havers crouched stiffly on a stretcher on the floor under the lights. They did not bear the slightest resemblance to anything human any more. They were an ugly heap of dirty rags.

"Contact shot," said the doctor, still brusquely but with a touch of surprise in his gruff baritone. "Three vertebrae dislodged, one shattered. Skull base cracked, multiple cerebral hemorrhages. Death instant. Sometime between five and seven hours ago. Do better for you later on that, when I've seen his stomach."

It was after 5:00 A.M. then. There was most of the county homicide squad and a restless, shuffling mob of news buzzards kibitzing over our shoulders. The Havers publicity jinx was right back on the job. Murder isn't such a hot undercover proposition.

"Hey, doc! You mean they jammed a gun into his neck, like these Nazis used to kill off prisoners?" inquired a brashly incredulous voice from their ranks.

I recognized the voice and subdued a grin, Sam Levy.

The doctor ignored him and continued working, but the florid old Irishman Hogan had introduced to me as Captain Vickers, in command of the homicide detail, turned around.

"Looks that way, boys," he boomed, almost triumphantly, as if he were doing them a big favor.

I was quietly glad I'd left the little woman waiting upstairs. The garage couldn't have competed successfully in comfort and charm of atmosphere with a clandestine slaughterhouse.

One of the men who'd been busily working over the Packard with a powder spray and a magnifying glass sidled up to Vickers and said, "Nothing doing, Cap'n. The heap's got more prints'n a playboy's got etchings, all of 'em in the wrong places. They used the off-side door and wiped the handle clean'n everything."

"Well, now you know," I said. "That let's us out. We wouldn't bother much wiping prints from our own door handle."

"Wouldn't you, mah boy?" said Vickers, laying on the heavy irony with a trowel.

"I've shot plenty of guys deader than that, but I was never shown how to sneak up behind them and put the blast on them like this. I'd feel silly!"

Vickers glowered at me, but Hogan nodded indifferently.

"We'll talk it over," he said, not unkindly. "Looks like they was after putting the hex on you two while they were about it, the old meanies. You ain't much in line for this, says my money."

The doctor climbed laboriously to his feet, rubbing a bloody towel over his beautiful hands and over something he held between two fingers.

"You want the slug now, Captain?" he inquired without curiosity.

"Yeah," said Vickers, heavily. "That we do, doc. Thanks."

The buzzards crowded around,

and we all had a peek at it together as he held it up under the floodlight. I had some little trouble restraining my whistle that wanted out. The bullet hadn't suffered much, because it was a nickel jacket from a high velocity autoloader. By rights it should have gone clean through and got lost, but some people have a lot of tough spine and gristle in their necks.

"That's .357 Magnum," Hogan said.

"Uh-huh."

Sam Levy was pulling at my sleeve, trying hard to take me aside from the crowd.

"What's your angle, Major?" he urged me in a desperate whisper. "You figure they're gonna pull you in on this? Who do you think done it? What goes on?"

"Sorry, Sam, no comment. Maybe some other time." I said behind the back of my hand.

"O.K., boys, that's all for now," Vickers was shouting. "We'll have more dope for you at headquarters in a couple of hours." He took Hogan's arm and pushed him along for a few steps, keeping me in focus with one glaring eye. They were arguing about me, I knew very well, and I watched Hogan's impassively skeptical profile remain impassively un-co-operative until he shook his head and jerked his thumb up at the ceiling, not injunctively but by manner of a strongly persuasive recommendation. The homicide man shrugged his shoulders and gave up.

"Come on!" he boomed at me. "What're we waiting for?"

Upstairs we found the little woman asleep on the divan. I had to wake her up and put her to work on the coffee machine and the sandwich material. I needed a drink, but somehow it seemed like a cold-blooded idea.

"Spit it out, Major," Hogan said sharply. "Where you've been all night and what you were up to. And you better remember we're out of the kindergarten class now. You lay it on the line, or we run the pair of you in as material witnesses anyway."

"Put it this way," I told him wearily. "You know I've been digging at people and things, trying to clear up that phony snatch. Late this afternoon I spoke to Fleming, Havers' public relations counsel, and he gave me to understand he was a bit suspicious of this guy Marescu . . ."

And so on and on. The stenographer had a marvelous do with it.

"O.K., we'll check on this just for the record," Hogan informed me. "I expect the D.A. will wanna have a little talk with you about it. That still leaves the main question wide open—when and where'd that body get into your car?"

"There's no way of making

sure, that I can see," I said ruefully. "If he was killed between ten and twelve, they might have palmed him off on me right here, before we left last night; we didn't use the car all day until about eleven-thirty, it was in the basement all the time, and I'm certain we never once looked in the back until we returned. But that would mean they knew where we lived, and anyway my guess is they carted him out to Sherman Oaks, meaning to dump the whole thing in Marescu's lap—they might even have mistaken my car for his while it was parked out front. Of course, it's just as possible he may actually be the lad himself; that Filipino butler of his had plenty of time to work the stunt while we were talking to him in the living room. And his gun could have been fired in the course of a row they had with young Havers, even if it isn't the gun that did the damage—that was a small Mauser I took away from him, but for all I know he's got a dozen more out there, including any number of .357 Magnums."

"We'll see about that," Vickers promised grudgingly, burying his large yellow teeth into a tongue on rye out of my icebox.

"But, Johnny, listen, *why* would anybody want to kill that poor boy?" my sweet little bride demanded. "Who are 'they' you all keep on talking about? I simply can't understand it. . . ."

Vickers fixed his suspicious red bug eyes on her, while Hogan and I consulted each other with a mutually wary glance.

"We're just guessing now, ma'am," said the confidential squad lieutenant, resuming his attention to the proper stirring of sugar in his coffee cup.

"It's like this, honeybee," I said uncomfortably. "We're inclined to believe what happened was that Lonny became worried, last Wednesday, when the pay-off misfired because of our intervention, and that she got in touch with Bob, her half brother, to seek his help and advice. Probably about the same time a real mob of crooks stumbled upon the game she was playing and decided to muscle in on it—the risks she was taking, she practically asked for something like that to occur, living in that neighborhood, monkeying around in barbershops and cheap restaurants. It may even have been that she discovered she was in danger, and then she didn't dare go back to her father or see the cops, and didn't want to go to her mother. That meant Bob would be her logical choice. He wasn't such a bad egg, only a bit mixed up, he'd be worth a try from her point of view. But however it was, they moved in and snatched her in earnest, and when Bob objected, he was given the business, perhaps because he saw or knew too much. Once they had his corpse on their hands, they might just as well have dumped it in the Pacific, but then they'd be likely to have heard of either Marescu or us as convenient potential suspects, so they took the trouble. It's awfully messy, but it makes sense, of a kind. . . ."

"Huh," said Vickers. "That would suit you good, now, wouldn't it? A pretty line that leaves you two high, dry, an' safe out of it. Only you ain't got a scrap of evidence to back it up with."

"You're so right, Captain," I said. "Now I'll tell one. You haven't got a scrap of evidence against *us* either, the way this deal's stacked. So I'm about to make a civil suggestion to you. Suppose you finish your coffee and drift the hell out of here and let us get some sleep."

He bridled at me, his big pugnacious Irish face flushing dark with indignation, but Hogan held up his hand in a wearily soothing gesture.

"No call for losing our temper," he admonished both of us, his tough gray features blankly dispassionate. "Could be Major Marshall's on the right track, and he's anyway entitled to make us put up or shut up on this. I'm not saying I'm satisfied, but I figure you and I ought to push off, Captain, and get to work."

We had ourselves half a minute or so of profound and dismal silence, with everybody endeavoring to outstare everybody else, and with doubtful speculation so thick in the air you could have pared it with a butter knife. Then Vickers shrugged his shoulders with exaggerated elaboration, as if he were now about to become a party to some extremely ill-advised and questionable deal. He drained his coffee cup and rose reluctantly to his feet, and immediately the room changed to a scene of much artificially jovial activity that involved the customary handshaking and polite smiling of a conventional departure of casual visitors.

"Not thinking of leaving town, are you, Major?" Hogan suggested on the doorstep. "And you'll remember what I told you about how we'll appreciate you not interfering with our business—"

"Or else," I helped him. "Don't worry, my friend. I'll remember."

When the door clicked shut behind them, the little woman came to bury her face in my shirt and to make subdued sounds of much relieved emotional distress. I used my arms around her in the manner prescribed by nature and ancient tradition for such contingencies, and squeezed, not quite hard enough to break all of her ribs.

"What did you expect, cherry pie? A rumba band to serenade you, and the mayor with a gold key to the city on a velvet cushion?"

"But it's all so *horrible*, Johnny.

I know we've been up against a lot of nasty things before, but at least they were done by people we could understand, because they were enemies and out to hurt us in every possible way. This is different somehow, these are our own people, and they do this just for money!"

"Yeah, and that surprises you, does it? They've been doing it all over the place, as long as I can remember. It only affects you because we happen to be sitting smack in the middle of one particular case. Otherwise you'd glance over it in a newspaper headline and pass it by to look for the comic-strip section, same way you get more upset over my scratching a fender than about news of a million dying in a Chinese famine. Got a kiss for me?"

And a few minutes later in bed, with just the top sheet to protect us from the fragrantly genial breeze of dawn floating in through the open windows, she snuggled up against me and whispered drowsily: "We're really terribly lucky, aren't we, sweet? Think of what might have happened, and if you hadn't been clever. . . ."

I had different views, but such faith should never be disillusioned, so I just grunted and pulled her closer, and rubbed gently behind her ears until she went to sleep.

It was again our Henry who woke us up on the telephone, Friday around noon. I could barely recognize his voice. There was no more than a trace left of his old breezy manner and vigorously cheerful intonation. He sounded badly rattled and much subdued.

"Sorry about all this, old boy," I said, as soon as we had established contact. "You know we meant well, but it looks like we're all up against it now. I wish you'd speak to Mr. Havers for me and tell him how much we regret what's happened—we'd do it ourselves, if we thought he could bear with us."

"Oh, that's all right, Major. The Sheriff's been here all morning, and every one of us is glad to learn you two are safe and in the clear. That, with Mrs. Havers' return, has been the only relief in this terrible tragedy."

"So Mrs. Havers has come back?" I said, mildly astonished.

"Yes, indeed. She rushed over immediately after she heard," he told me with some of the old enthusiasm. "Isn't it remarkable, though, the wonderful way misfortune has of reconciling personal differences and drawing people together? I think there's every possibility now that they may make up for keeps and see it through together. Listen, Major, whatever did happen to you last night? Lieutenant Hogan gave me some of it, and he asked me about our conversation yesterday, but I couldn't make sense out of it all."

"I hope you didn't tell him about our private arrangements," I said. "We figured we'd better try to protect you on that angle, so I never mentioned we'd been in touch with you before yesterday."

"Gosh, I didn't know how to put it myself," he confessed. "That certainly was swell of you, Major. I thought you'd probably have managed, so I just said you'd called me to ask for information, and since I'd always been convinced you were on the up and up, I talked to you about my suspicions of our friend M. And then he explained to me that I must have given you a bum steer, but I still can't understand how."

"It doesn't matter now. You're O.K. as far as your boss and Hogan are concerned; it never occurred to him to associate you with this apartment, he thinks we made a sublease deal with the regular tenant."

"Oh, grand! Look, Major, to heck with subleases and all that stuff. You two stay right where you are, if it suits you there, until you can find a place of your own. There's this terrible housing shortage here in L. A.; it'll take you weeks to get a decent roof over your heads."

"That's neighborly of you, Henry," I said, more or less gratefully. "We'd appreciate that a lot, if it won't inconvenience you too much. How's Hogan getting along, any progress? He was going after

my pal with the silky side whiskers when he left here early this morning."

"I don't know . . . ," he said uncertainly, hesitating for several seconds before he went on. "There's so much, er, confusion here, so much conflict of ideas and theories, and I've been busy all the time keeping the reporters at bay, so to speak. And then there's still our, er, agreement to be considered. I wish you'd let me off on that, Major, I really do! If I had realized how much I'd be on the spot when I promised you—"

"So there is news!" I snapped. "Don't tell me you've received instructions for another pay-off?"

I could hear him catch at his breath, but in any case the silence after that gave me plenty of answer.

"It's O.K., Henry," I said soothingly. "We've quit the game, we won't interfere anymore. We're just interested bystanders now, you don't have to go through with it if it embarrasses you. Where you talking from, the bungalow?"

"Yes, surely. There's not a moment's privacy at the house, and they've bugged up all the wires there now, since the call came in at nine this morning. It's not that I'm, uh, embarrassed, Major. I guess you might as well hear this, so long as you're not going to do anything."

"Phoned, did they?" I observed grimly. "Well, that's something for the book! Those boys have a nerve."

"Margaret took the call," he told me, still hesitating. "It came in on the direct wire to her office, the same one you were on last Tuesday when you wanted me. The man had a sneering manner and a cheap, hard voice, she said, obviously a crude type.

"She had the presence of mind to take it all in shorthand, nervous as she was. I've got a copy of it here, I'll read it to you."

He coughed, and I heard the crackle of paper.

"This is how she typed it up," he said.

"TIME: 9.04 A.M., call on switchboard line number one. MISS RENSHAW: 'Mr. Wilton Havers' secretary speaking.'
CALLER: 'O.K., sister, you know who this is. I got a message for you.'
MISS RENSHAW: 'Oh, yes, sir, if you'd wait a moment, I'm sure Mr. Havers will want to speak with you himself.'
CALLER: '——(terribly rude and vulgar expression) your boss, I ain't waiting for nobody. Get this, sister. We're holding that brat of his, see, and he can either kick through with that two hundred and fifty grand now or we'll ship her to him in just that many pieces, get me?'
MISS RENSHAW: 'Yes, yes, I

understand. Please don't harm her; I know Mr. Havers will pay you and do as you want him to.'
CALLER: 'O.K., sister, keep your shirt on.' (Laughs and says off receiver: 'Whadda you think? The dame's already wetting her pants.') 'O.K., take this down. Tell Havers to be alone in a station wagon at Slauson and La Tijera at four tomorrow afternoon sharp. We'll count time by the L. A. telephone clock, see? Tell him to stick a sheet of white paper on the right corner of his windshield and wait there with all his doors open. At four-fifteen he can close the doors and roll, down La Tijera and Sepulveda to Ocean Boulevard, and on 101A to San Diego. Tell him to go thirty all the way, and turn left on state 54 past San Juan Capistrano for twenty miles, turn back, go south again on 101, turn left on state 89 off Solano Beach for fifteen miles, turn back, go north to L.A. on 101, turn right on 54 again for twenty miles, go back to Slauson and La Tijera the way he came out. Got all that?'
MISS RENSHAW: 'Yes, sir. Shall I read it back?'
CALLER: '——(very vulgar word) on that, whatsamatter with you, sister, you think I got time for that kind of malarkey? Tell Havers to watch for the

green signal we'll give him, short-long-short-long, like that, he'll get it O.K. He stops right there, dumps the dough in a bag on one side of the road, turns around, and gets the hell out of there, fast as he can make it, see? Tell him we're keeping an eye on him all the way, and he better have no cops or any cute ideas like marking bills on this if he wants the brat back. That's the dope, sister.'

"Nice fellows," I said, dropping the pencil I had used to jot down a few notes. "Well, all I can say is I hope Havers has sense enough to let the Sheriff tackle this and to give him a free hand on it. I'd sure love to pitch in and grab me a share of these monkeys, but my pal Hogan didn't seem to approve somehow, and anyway he's probably equal to the occasion himself all right. Thanks for calling me, Henry, and thanks again for helping us out with the apartment and everything. You come on up and have dinner with us when this has blown over."

That would be fine, he admitted, he'd like that very much, but now he really ought to run and get back on the job, and please to give his best regards to Mrs. Marshall.

That young lady had been hanging over my shoulder for several minutes, trying to listen in and scanning my pencil notes.

"It's bad, Johnny, isn't it? What do you make of it?"

"Sure it's bad, we found that out last night, didn't we? The pay-off method's typically professional now, about as foolproof as you can make it—just as I told you, a lonely road somewhere and a signal to drop the bundle when they're satisfied the coast is clear. The setup's hard to beat, but do you realize what makes it all much worse?"

"Yes, I think I see what you mean," she said, frowning unhappily. "It's Bob's murder, isn't it? That must make a big difference to them."

"You're not just kidding. It makes all the difference in the world. They didn't go out of their way to kill him, but they must have been in a fix: he saw them, he showed fight, they were in a hurry, it was a question of giving up altogether and losing a fortune or putting the freeze on him. Now they're playing for keeps. Their only chance is to collect and do a fast fade-out to Guatemala or Ecuador or some place. They've got reserved seats in the San Quentin gas chamber anyway, so a killing more or less doesn't matter now, and dead bodies are often easier to manage than live ones."

"Oh, darling, you're thinking of Lonny."

"Lonny might be kind of hard to manage," I had to point out. She began to cry, and I put my arms around her and tried to comfort her; awkwardly, because there was so little comfort to be had, and because I was reproaching myself at the same time for letting her in on my gloomy ideas.

"But isn't there anything we can *do?*" she sobbed.

"Honey lamb, it's up to Lieutenant Hogan and his crowd," I said regretfully, petting her ears. "At least they have all the facts now, and they'll have to give it the business. This is a murder case, and even if Havers wanted to fix the pay-off again, they couldn't play with him. It would all come out eventually, and the public would never stand for it. There's nothing for us but to let them handle it—"

There was a knock on the door of the apartment. After a moment's hesitation, I got up and walked over to see, while Suzy, dabbing at her eyes, fled to the bedroom for repairs.

"Please forgive me," said Alice Havers, uncertainly. "I didn't mean to intrude, but I had to see you."

CHAPTER 9

I HASTILY buttoned the jacket over the manly chest and stumbled aside in a gawky attempt at the prescribed courtly gesture.

"Come right in, please, Mrs. Havers," I said, disciplining my larynx severely. "If you'll pardon me for receiving you like this. We were up pretty late this, uh, morning."

She didn't hesitate, she walked right by me into the living room, took the chair I was proffering with another clumsy flourish of my lily-white hand, and started fumbling in her bag for cigarettes. I mustered a match for her, and she relaxed a little.

Suzy came hurrying in from the bathroom, zippering her housecoat, auburn curls still flying over her shoulders, and I performed the introduction. It took them all of twenty minutes to express their mutual sympathies and recriminations.

I sat by patiently, watching, smoking, and listening to our visitor's distracted account of the fateful telephone instructions, until at last the expected pass at my conscience materialized, in an unexpected manner.

"Please, Major Marshall, don't misunderstand, but won't you help us? If I had only known you when you came to see me. . . ."

"So you were actually aware at the time of Lonny's little prank, were you?" I said mildly. "You'd had that call from your husband before I arrived? Frankly, Mrs. Havers, I can hardly believe it would have made much difference. I'm willing to take it for granted that you'd have returned the money and assisted in correcting the child if she had brought it off according to plan, but I don't quite see you trusting in me at the time to the extent of telling me the story and helping me to find her. After all, you didn't even bother to tell your husband, you let him go on believing she'd been taken by crooks!"

She had herself carefully under control now, but her eyes continued to avoid me.

"I was angry with him," she said. "I thought it might teach him a lesson, jolt him out of his horrible self-complacency. Of course, I didn't realize he was going to pay and keep the police from interfering. He did not tell me that, and I had no idea Lonny would go as far as she did, or that she was in any real danger—don't you *see* how it had to look to me? She was only a baby being naughty for a day or two, until she'd be caught by a big fatherly policeman who'd bawl her out and take her home again. . . ."

"Darling, that's not unreasonable," Suzy urged me.

I wasn't prepared to argue the point, but I didn't think it covered the field. Women are strange creatures of the Lord; you always have to count on a certain amount of reverse English in their ideas and emotions. It occurred to me that perhaps our Alice had not been altogether as anxious to secure a divorce as she had made out, that she had hoped and considered the incident might lead the Boss to discover that she was an indispensable factor in the family, and to mend his ways accordingly.

"Well, it just goes to show," I said righteously. "Any time you look for somebody else to get a jolt, things have a funny way of turning around and jolting right back at you. I'm sorry, Mrs. Havers, but I can't help."

"If it's a question of money . . . ," she said hesitantly, in a small voice.

I shrugged my shoulders, keeping both irony and annoyance out of my face with some difficulty.

"It is not a question of money," I said carefully. "There's a very nice check in my pocket right now that was offered to me by someone anxious to protect the interests of your family. I'm mailing it back today. It's not easy to see why you should even ask me, Mrs. Havers. We haven't accomplished very much in the past few days, to put it mildly."

"You're still cross with me. Because I called you stupid and because I said I was going to have your wife testify under a subpoena," she said desperately. "Please, Major, I didn't really mean it, won't you believe that? Lieutenant Hogan told me you've had a lot of experience dealing with gangsters, in army counter-intelligence . . ." She suddenly took her eyes away from me and buried them in her long, graceful hands. Suzy came over to her and put an arm around her. I shifted uncomfortably in my chair.

"I'm sorry," I said again, beginning to feel like a cracked phonograph record. "It can't be done. If Hogan told you that, he also told you I have no license to operate as a private investigator and that he warned me off the case under threats of arrest. This has got to a point where only a lot of organization and equipment and teamwork can do any good. Does your husband know about your visit here, Mrs. Havers?"

She shook her head miserably, and I said with the impatience of a squirrel who's been cracking empty nuts all day: "Well, is there anything you know or anything you're guessing at that you haven't given to the Sheriff? What about Bob, have you any ideas where he was killed or how he got involved? After all, even if I were in a position to act, we'd have to have something to work on. . . ."

Another headshake.

Suzy said, "I wonder how they killed him so easily, without getting damaged themselves. That dog should have caused them a lot of trouble. Do you think it was shot, too? If we could find that out. . . ."

The point had occurred to me,

and I had dismissed it from my mind just as promptly. Dogs could bark and bite, but I didn't think they were much use against a couple of hard-boiled hoodlums. I shrugged my shoulders again, and then Alice said dully, "Khan's gone. He ran away Tuesday afternoon, according to the servants, and he never came back. Bob didn't disappear until after dinner on Thursday."

"That's odd," I said. "He was Bob's private property, wasn't he? Not especially devoted to Lonny or anything, so he'd go looking for her?"

Before she could reply, the door was being knocked on again. We were getting to be the most popular couple in Hollywood, now that everybody knew where we could be found, I thought wryly, going over to see.

Hogan walked in on us, deadpan as ever, very politely doffing his hat to the ladies. He gave no sign of surprise when he recognized our visitor, not so much as a twitch of the furrowed brow.

"Have you folks had your breakfast yet?" he inquired matter-of-factly, without any special interest or good cheer.

I told him no, and felt mildly inclined to slap him on the back. Alice Havers heard and took the cue, departing in a flurry of conventional apologies and brightly embarrassed smiles. I transferred my stare from the door as it closed behind her to the gray-faced stoic across the room and said, "You want to watch out, shocking us like that. We might faint or something. A solicitous cop!"

"Not up to your old tricks again, Major, digging at people?" he asked me frostily, ignoring my innocent sally.

I grinned at him, but Suzy flared out of the room and slammed the kitchen door in girlish protest.

"No offense," he said calmly. "I kinda figured Mrs. Havers might think to pay you a call, she was asking so many questions about you. Well, we're all set, Major. Thought you'd like to know. They're not going to get away with this one."

"So the Boss'll play ball with *you* now, will he?" I said.

"You can call it that if you like. He ain't got much choice in it. He's gonna take that trip to San Diego and back tomorrow afternoon. I suppose she told you all about it?"

He saw my nod and coughed significantly.

"How do you reckon they aim to bring it off?" he wanted to know.

"You need *me* to tell you!" I said sarcastically. "They make Havers travel two or three hundred miles, some of it over roads that have no more than half a dozen farmers' trucks on them on an average day. They've got a fast car or God knows maybe a light plane parked in a handy place; all they need to do is wait for him on a hilltop near by, spot his station wagon from a mile away with glasses, and shoot him the code with a strong flash or with one of these portable airfield signal lamps with a beam you can use like a rifle. He stops and lets go of the bundle, they can swoop down on it and be off to Mexico in five minutes flat."

"Bills will all be invisibly marked, of course," he said. "Sodium naphthionate, shows up instantly under black light, standard procedure; every bank, post office, race track will crack down on 'em. Don't mean much if they'd get away south and play it smart, but we don't aim to let them do it. Be a dragnet on for them all the way down to the border and as far east as Yuma and Las Vegas on every road, in every county. We got a couple dozen prowl cars on this job, staked out pretty, so they'll never be more than five or ten minutes away from Havers. We're putting a radio in his car; the minute he delivers he's to give us the word, and we'll close in on these bunnies and have them cornered."

Suzy entered with a trayload of orange juice, scrambled eggs, bacon, toasted buns, and three cups of coffee. She looked flushed from the stove heat and charmingly disarranged in appearance, but she had squeezed in a layer of lipstick somewhere between chores.

"So you're going to catch them," she said contemptuously. "I suppose you have to do it, so they won't go and kidnap some more people. But what about that poor girl? What did you think will happen to *her,* when you surround those mobsters while they're holding her?"

"There's always that," I said reasonably. "Either she's already dead and they're on a double cross for the ransom, or she's alive, in which case they might do her in when they're trapped, but chances are they wouldn't. It's seconds that count in a trap like that, why should they bother wasting even a few to satisfy their vindictiveness at the expense of their chances to break out of the trap?"

"Johnny, there must be another way. Something to forestall them, find out where they're hiding her before tomorrow afternoon, so they can be taken while they're off guard. Couldn't that phone call have been traced? Isn't it possible to check on her movements while she was still on her own, last Wednesday?"

"We try, ma'am," said Hogan, bringing his candid blue eyes to bear on her, like twin battleship guns being exercised empty in a peacetime drill. "We ain't doing so well, though," he added calmly. "Call was made in the Santa Monica zone, didn't pass through no operator, so there's no record of it. It's next to impossible to trace dialed calls, and there's too many public boxes anyway. We've had lots of men out since Wednesday already, working on the kid's movements. She never come back to that job of hers in the barbershop after lunch. We got Cattano and his wife in custody, the janitors at her place—they say she phoned a few minutes after you were gone, and they told her what happened. She didn't say anything, Cattano claims, she just hung up and they never saw her any more. They also claim they had no idea what was in the bag until it was opened by Kennedy at your suggestion. We're digging around the joint, looking for characters she might have been tipped to; no luck so far. I'm going back there myself now. Thought I'd stop by here to see if you were happy . . ."

"And toeing the line," I finished for him. "Considerate of you, Lieutenant. We thought you came to talk about a guy who's been firing Mauser pistols in his garden to keep in practice. I gather you didn't do so well with him either."

He didn't like that. The blue eyes came around to me, slightly cloudy and puzzled to vexation.

"You got second sight," he said slowly, without even a pinch of sarcasm. "You must of been born with the helmet, Major. That wouldn't be your second breakfast today after all, would it? And by the way, Mr. Havers swears he never did make no pass at the lady here, like you said happened. That faze you any?"

It was a question of grin and bear it. The Marescu angle didn't really fit in anywhere that I could see—not any more at that point. The way it turned out, there was some more reverse English on it, but we were all of us so preoccupied with the grim and startling main issues that I frankly don't believe it would have done us much good if we could have spotted it, because we were almost bound to have missed the implications. I was satisfied Hogan had searched and probed and grilled, that he had found reasons and alibis, that he would detail men to watch and probe further, if that were necessary. And any connection there might have been between Marescu and Alice Havers had lost its meaning to me now, for what it might have been worth in the first place.

"Thanks for the coffee," Hogan said from our doorway, in a voice that meant just that and no more.

We spent the next twenty-four hours in almost idyllic isolation.

We did some shopping, ate our meals, and walked to a double-feature movie in Westwood Village on Friday evening; we slept, after a fashion, that night and used up the predictable quantity and quality of highly confused dreams. The car itself had been taken away for laboratory examination, but it was returned to us in fair condition by a police headquarters mechanic on Saturday morning. Most of the time we managed somehow to avoid any further and so obviously fruitless discussion of the whole uncomfortable subject.

The fact that our restlessness increased as the Saturday afternoon dead line approached could hardly be ascribed to the visions of second sight, the way Hogan appeared willing to allow for them.

We lunched without much appetite off some cold cuts and potato salad at one-thirty on Saturday, and afterward we could only hang around the apartment, getting under each other's feet and on each other's nerves, like a couple of difficult children convalescing from the measles but still under house arrest. I had half a mind to sally forth and drive over the San Diego route myself, in the role of a law-abiding but curious citizen availing himself of his undeniable privilege to travel on the public highways and to see what goes on there. But there was the possibility of causing confusion and delay to be reckoned with, strong enough to make the idea altogether too irresponsible.

Not many hours later there were moments when I had some reason to regret these earlier statesmanlike scruples.

That day's especially messy and devilish firecracker of events started sizzling at three-thirty in the afternoon, when the phone broke into a shrill tattoo right against the small of my back where I was sitting on the table, smoking a cigarette and minding my own business. It made me jump fit to graze the ceiling. Suzy came running in from the bedroom, and for a while we just stood there, looking doubtfully at each other and at the stubbornly noisy instrument.

"Want me to answer it?" I asked her finally, with the air of a bank cashier inspecting a clumsy sample of counterfeit.

"I don't know . . ." she said hesitantly, and almost bumped into me when we both suddenly reached for the receiver together.

The dry, placid old man's voice of Mr. Earl G. Spencer came over the wire, colorless and unhurried.

"Your note returning my check to me was received by my office this morning," he said. "I appreciate your correct attitude toward me in the matter."

"Oh," I managed, not without some difficulty. "The check . . . sure thing. Yeah. Of course."

"May one presume that the case as such is still a subject of personal interest to you?" he inquired, so indifferently that my ears flapped right back up to attention.

"One may indeed," I assured him, as heartily as I could.

"I find myself confronted by the urgent necessity of reaching an exceedingly invidious decision," he told me. "I'm speaking from the Havers ranch, and my client departed on his mission a few minutes ago. I understand you are acquainted with its purpose, or perhaps I should say its avowed purpose, since the suitcase he carries is, er, empty."

There seemed to be no point in whistling like a high-school boy getting a load of the facts of life. I sat down in the nearest chair, blew a perfectly round smoke ring and maintained an expectant silence. The little woman, seeing my face, promptly nestled in my lap and pressed an ear close to the phone.

"The situation is so utterly without precedent," crackled the high, dry voice, "that I am practically at a loss for its proper remedy. However, I would wish to secure your opinion and possibly your assistance."

"Perhaps we can meet you somewhere," I suggested.

"There is no time for that now, I'm afraid. I must confess to my dislike of the telephone as a medium for confidential communication, but there is no option under the circumstances. At three o'clock my client received a call on the private line in his study from the person or persons who are claiming to hold Miss Havers. He was informed in crude language that these people had realized, when they formulated their original instructions to him, the physical impossibility of withholding these instructions from the authorities, and the consequent inevitability of vigorous official reaction to them. They chose to assume, however, that he would still desire to co-operate with them by paying ransom in accordance with fresh and secret instructions, thus circumventing police measures they knew to have been taken. This assumption was backed by the customary threats and by a reminder of the manner of Robert Havers' death."

"And he agreed?" I demanded, burying nails in my palms.

"Yes, I am afraid he did. I was closeted in conference with him at the time, and I may say I made every attempt to dissuade him, but perhaps he should not be blamed for allowing his better judgment to be overruled by high anxiety over his daughter's life. As it was, he undertook to proceed to San Diego on the original schedule, to mislead the police, and to dispatch the ransom money by a trusted messenger over a totally different route."

"O.K.," I said. "What's the new route, and who's going?"

"Mr. Fleming reluctantly volunteered to deliver the money when my client sent for him and informed him of the situation. He is to leave here at four o'clock and

to proceed north toward San Francisco on the ocean-front highway. As I understand it, there is a note with further instructions waiting for him at a Shell Company filling station one mile south of Oxnard. The note will be addressed to Mr. John F. Jones, to be called for."

He paused, waiting for my reaction. I could have used a pause, too, about six hours of one. Suzy was whispering excitedly in my unoccupied ear, but I didn't hear a word of that, I was concentrating so hard on trying to make the spinning little wheels stop and fit into a sensible pattern.

"Fleming agrees with you that Havers is off the beam on this, does he?" I asked.

"Certainly!" he came back, sharply. "However, I must admit that under the circumstances he is obviously the best available man to carry out this deplorable assignment. If we had any assurance that these criminals are actually holding Miss Havers alive, and that they intend to free her upon receiving payment—"

"Yeah, I know. Well, it's probably too late now to warn the cops on this anyway," I said. "They're all set on the wrong foot, a hundred miles or more south of where this show will play. Is Fleming with you there?"

"Yes, he is prepared to leave."

I had the map open before me and glanced at my watch.

"It's three-forty-nine now," I

said. "Get him to synchronize. The filling station's a little over fifty miles from here, about forty-three from where you are. Tell him to push off at four sharp and not drive too fast, so I can catch up with him. He's to hit the filling station at five-fifteen on the nose and go on from there to wherever the note says, making sure I can trail him. What kind of car's he taking?"

There was a brief palaver at the other end before the dry old voice returned with the desired intelligence.

"Forest-green Cadillac convertible," I repeated. "O.K., Mr. Spencer, tell him to act natural and let them expect just the one man who'll follow their orders, but to be ready to jump them with me, the minute they try to accept delivery. He looks like a useful customer in a scrap; the two of us can take them by surprise."

He started to mumble something about admiration and personal courage, but I slammed the phone and made a grab for my coat and hat, only to find a hundred and fifteen pounds of strong and determined young woman hanging on my arm.

"No, you don't, Johnny! Either I go along, or I call the cops—"

"The viper I have nursed in my bosom," I protested bitterly, knowing her well enough to realize she wasn't fooling. "You'll be sorry, Suze. There's a nasty rough-house coming up, on account of I am getting seriously displeased with these monkeys."

"Come on, we'd better hurry," she told me flatly.

She ran ahead of me down the stairs to the basement, lithe and slender in her blue slacks and summer sweater, the long red curls rushing out to make her appear like a reasonable facsimile of a dark Valkyrie riding off to battle. Her grandmother Willett used to think nothing of fighting a band of marauding Indians with an ax and a hunting knife, I remembered uncomfortably. We had been in a brawl or two together before, with very satisfactory results, but they never failed to inflict injury on my sense of proportions and of decent masculine prerogative.

The old Packard responded with a happy roar to my touch on the starter button, as if it considered carrying a pair of zanies who proposed to go after an undetermined number of murderers and kidnapers with their bare hands the life of Reilly for an old Packard. It raced us out on Wilshire, slipping past the lights where opportunity availed, hit Santa Monica with its engine nicely warmed up, and started burning off the ocean speedway miles on a northern course.

We overtook the green Cadillac a few miles beyond Malibu, sizzled past it, and kept on going.

The Shell filling station turned out to be a big, modern six-pump affair in the southern outskirts of the town of Oxnard, on the continental side of the highway where it skirted the beach in a wide curve. We swept by at four-fifty-seven and swung into the driveway of an only slightly less impressive Texaco competitor, about a block and a half up the road.

There was a good deal of traffic, and the air was heavy with exhaust fumes and the smell of rubber on hot asphalt, barely stirred by a faint and salty breeze where it drifted in from the quietly murmuring Pacific. The day had been pleasantly warm, but by then the sun was beginning to lose interest and occasionally taking time out behind a capricious screen of white cumulus that moved lazily across the western horizon. Over the endless range of yellow hills, the afternoon sky's royal blue had already faded to a smokier shade.

We sat in the car, waiting patiently while the colored attendant pumped in gas and checked the oil and performed about ten minutes' worth of all the little routine chores I could think up for him. We had a fair picture of the Shell station and kept a close eye on it; in spite of the constant whirr of traffic, it was doing only desultory business, and none of that seemed inclined to linger. There were no convenient buildings near by, and no cars parked within rifleshot. If this was supposed to be a check point, from the snatchers' point of view, it did not look like a very efficient one, unless they had a tie-up with one of the attendants, which was always a reasonable possibility.

"Be a dollah ninety-one, please, suh."

I tipped the boy a quarter. He was a handsome, alert young Negro with a wise, happy smile and gleaming white teeth; I was tempted to ask him if he knew of any recently employed staff in the Shell outfit down the road, but the question would have marked us immediately—we couldn't afford the slightest risk of appearing conspicuous; we might almost as well have traveled right into the other station and inquired for the note to Mr. John F. Jones ourselves. It was only twelve minutes past five, and I started talking to the boy about buying some new tires. He took exactly three minutes to tell me he might get some in next week, or maybe not before January.

At five-fifteen on the dot, the green Cadillac detached itself from the northbound traffic stream and idled into the Shell lot to park beside the glassed-in sales office. Even at that distance it was easy to recognize our Henry's hatless, beautifully groomed taffy hair and the swing of his tall, well-knit figure striding away from his car into the office, without hesitating or looking around. He stood in conversation with the station manager for only a few seconds, his back toward us. We were too far away to see what passed between them, but when he came out there was the white flutter of an envelope in his hands.

He climbed into the Cadillac, swiveled leisurely around, and eased onto the highway, turning back south toward Los Angeles, merging in the steady buzz of traffic.

I let the Packard drift away from its Texaco pump in the same general direction, while we both scanned the road again and again in a concentrated attempt to spot possible tracers. Fifteen minutes and some nine miles later I became morally convinced there were none. Nobody else wanted to travel quite so conservatively. Cars kept on flashing by at fifty or sixty all the time, but not a single one of them dawdled behind or just ahead. The Cadillac and we passed an occasional slow truck; most of the time it was dead simple to keep an average distance of two hundred yards between us. I began to wish Henry would hurry up a bit. We might have a long ride ahead of us for all I knew, and darkness was at best a dubious advantage for our plans.

Once or twice I nearly made up my mind to overtake him and confer on strategy, but each time the fear of a running checkup held me back. We were taking plenty of chances anyway, but the sight of our cars pulled up together and of the three of us in palaver by the roadside would have been just too ducky, if our friends should have decided to patrol the route once or twice.

By six-thirty we were back in the Malibu sector and still jogging south at a steady thirty-five. It was getting much cooler now, and the sun was already dunking its lower rim in the ocean, but the beach was still gay with colored umbrellas, and the surf full of squealing and scurrying bathers.

"Darling, look! He's turning left!"

Henry had suddenly slowed down to a crawl, and his arm was waving out of the window. The green convertible sliced through oncoming traffic and made a dash for a narrow side road into the hills.

"Fair enough," I said, hanging back for a few seconds to allow for space and appearances before urging the Packard on the same course.

The side road wasn't even signposted, but it had the number 117 up on a small white metal plaque, tacked on a telephone pole at the intersection. It was a narrow, second-grade macadam county road, the type that will accommodate two cars at a time, if their fenders are smoothly polished. Right away we needed second gear, and the first bend took us out of sight from the beach.

We caught a glimpse of the Cadillac around the fourth hairpin after that, and a mile or so later we saw it again, edging off the road into what looked at that distance like a stretch of virgin digger pine.

I slapped the brakes on and backed quickly out of range. We hopped out to reconnoiter on foot, but our error soon became obvious. The green convertible was already through the pines and crawling down into a sage-grown valley on some sort of dirt track.

"Not so good," I said grudgingly.

This was jungle country, nothing but row upon row of thickly matted hills, with no farms or houses or any sign of normal human occupation for miles. Dusk was beginning to make itself at home, and a regiment of camouflage-trained infantry would have found no trouble hiding there, but an unexpected car was something else again.

"But Johnny, he *knows* we're behind him. He'd stop and tip us off if he thought we should walk."

"Yeah, if he dared. Well, we'll push on up that track anyway. Maybe he left a message."

We went back to our car and found the track. It was only a little more narrow than the road itself, but quite rough—unimproved gravel sand, carelessly graded and generously supplied with potholes. A painted steel chain between two short white poles marked it as closed to the enterprising public. There was no sign of any message, but the chain had been left ostentatiously unhooked, and the deep twin grooves made by the Cadillac's broad tires ran on past it without wavering. I saw other grooves, older and less impressive, difficult to appraise at a glance. The Cadillac itself had disappeared now, but we could still hear the hollow rumble of its engine in the distance.

"Sounds like he's going places," I said. "Well, last one in's a sissy."

Second gear was no use on that track, and first was still dangerously high. Some of its grades would have made an old Missouri mule pause for refreshment and contemplation. The old Packard groaned and snarled, staggering up and down this nightmare roller coaster, springs and clutch straining to their limit, motor laboring like a sick and weary galley slave. After the first few hundred yards I realized we were on a firebreak, just a bare trail through the mountains cut to stop brush fires and never intended to carry anything less formidable than a Sherman tank. It was not a comforting realization. Some firebreaks will last for a hundred miles or more.

Then we passed through the

fence, a trim low double-wire affair with an open gate to let us in. There are a lot of fences like that in the world, but this one couldn't fail to remind us. We treated each other to a whistle and a startled glance or two, and I almost forgot to keep my foot bearing down on the gas.

"Johnny, it *can't* be!"

"Oh, yes, it is," I said grimly. "Seventy-five hundred acres of it, clear down to the beach, remember? That county road crosses Lucerne Canyon somewhere, I've noticed it before, now that I come to think of it. We're on the less desirable part of the Havers estate, beautiful. These boys had a bright idea. They want the bundle delivered in the Boss's own back yard, where nobody would ever think to look for them."

We crawled painfully up another bushy hill, and we had almost reached the top when I made a dive for the brakes. The green Cadillac was parked empty at a drunken slue in a copse of holly brush off the track, just around the last zigzag, its rear bumper grazing my fender. The Packard's engine died in a loud gurgle of relief.

"End of the line, it seems," I said, jerking my thumb at a small eucalyptus grove above us, where the rough wood of a log cabin showed between the trees.

"Darling, we're in a spot. They must've heard us—they can even see us from there! What'll we *do?*"

"Can't be as bad as all that," I reassured her cheerfully. "They're not much likely to be up there now; they'd be silly to show their mugs to the messenger. This is just the dumping place, they might not even be watching it. We'll go up for a confab with our faithful Henry, and then we'll all have to pull out of here and lay a trap somehow. He's probably more or less familiar with this neck of the woods. We'll work out something."

We hopped out and started climbing the slope to the cabin. I didn't really feel so happy about it all. It was becoming embarrassingly evident that we were up against tactics much more brazenly resourceful than one usually comes across in dealing with the average criminal.

The log cabin was a pretty old and dilapidated shack of coarse gray timber, commanding a view of several miles of surrounding mountain jungle and at that moment receiving the last benefits of a rapidly fading crimson sunset. It had probably served its time as a fire watchers' observation post, but little evidence of such occupation remained; roof and walls sagged badly, every one of the small square windows was broken and carelessly boarded up. The tiny wooden porch looked dangerously unreliable. We crossed it with two or three cautious steps, felt the rickety front door give to our touch, and walked in, just as blithely as country folks from Osh-kosh, Wisconsin, come to call on the new neighbors with a batch of home-cooked corn muffins.

"Well, I'll be damned!" I allowed, stopping short, but much too bewildered to be really alarmed as yet.

The cabin's one big room was equipped with a few sticks of broken packing-case furniture, a brand-new mattress stacked with blankets in one corner, and a new Sears Roebuck type kerosene lamp burning brightly on the mantelpiece over the chimney. A disorderly array of canned provisions, fruit, and the remnants of a loaf of bread lay heaped around the kitchen sink. Books and magazines had been flung about here and there, and a small portable radio stood on the floor by the bed, gently drooling a Strauss waltz.

Miss Lorna Mae Havers sat on the bed, smoking a cigarette, perfectly composed. She was still wearing her cheap blue cretonne, but the pale honey bleach of her hair was already turning discouraged, and she had discarded her sleazy stockings in favor of white bobby socks. She looked exactly like a wise and self-sophisticated little high-school girl getting ready to be arch with a boy friend or two.

A large and familiar appearing airplane suitcase, the obvious twin of our original quarry, stood solidly on the floor at her dainty little feet. Beside it were planted two more feet, not nearly so dainty although pleasantly elegant in dusty oxblood sport shoes. Mr. Henry Fleming in his trimly expensive, coffee-brown gabardine suit, smiling upon us with his clear wide winsome eyes and confronting us with the business end of a large and shiny black .357 Magnum pistol.

CHAPTER 10

"WELL, WELL, if it isn't our Henry," I said, "the P.R.C. himself. Henry, I really gave you credit for more sense than this. I grant that this will give you a headline six inches high and more publicity than you ever dreamed of, but, Henry, m'boy, have you considered the sort of publicity it will be? The Boss isn't going to like this side of your nature, Henry. I'm surprised at you. And I must say that isn't a particularly glad hand you are holding out there. The gladioli you had in it for Suzy when you welcomed us before looked much gladder."

He laughed at me. Not politely, or heartily, more like a young and good-natured bank president listening to a small boy's application for a ten-dollar loan to set him up a soda-pop counter. I didn't feel so funny myself, or so very good-natured either. It was just a question of mechanically shooting off my mouth to gain a little time in which to digest all that rich heavy food for thought the situation was cramming down my gullet.

"No, sir, Major," he confessed candidly. "I fear the welcome I have for you this time, while warm, isn't quite in the same class." He laughed some more, he was so amused. "Flowers I should have provided, though. Very thoughtless of me," he added to his final snicker.

He had me there. We'd been too happy with him, too sure of him all along; the very idea of this nice, handsome, eager-to-please young lad in the function of a slithy tove crawling through the wabe had always bluntly refused to introduce itself to us. I was catching on fast now, somewhat belatedly. They have a trick in the movies sometimes of throwing the film into reverse to show you the diver jumping back out of the pool to his perch on the diving board. It never fails to score a howl, and it never will. I'd have given my right arm to be that diver then.

If he hadn't come out with the gun, he might easily have gone right on convincing us for a little while yet. But not for long enough to swing the deal, he knew that.

He hadn't counted on Spencer's bright idea of switching us in on it. He'd never even been aware of our contact with Spencer. Good old Spencer was supposed to be a member in excellent standing of the Havers society of fixers and tame politicians. He was definitely not supposed to kick over the traces and make life difficult for promising young murderers.

It was all very awkward, everything considered.

I didn't care for the gun so much. He might not be such a crack shot, but .357 is a nasty caliber, and six or seven feet isn't much of a distance to miss in.

"So you found my cigar butt, did you?" I said bleakly, sliding one tentative foot forward.

"Hold it, Major!" he snapped, dropping his smile. "Step back there, will you please!"

I gave him a worried, apologetic frown and stepped back quickly. It isn't difficult to trip, doing that, and the idea is to relax your shoulder muscles so they won't bruise when you hit the deck. It goes against the grain to shoot at a guy when he's having a silly accident like that, flopping on his fanny: the right psychology is half a second of mixed sympathy and *Schadenfreude*, and half a second is plenty of time to kick in. I kicked at the gun, high and hard.

It was a fair try. One does better in gymnasium practice, when the gun isn't loaded and you have a nice soft mat to fall on. The gun spat at the roof, roaring harmlessly, and sailed through the air in a pretty parabola. I didn't wait to see where it landed. I stuck my disengaged leg between his and twisted sideways, as they teach you in school, and he came down to join me on the floor with a crash.

That was the easy part of it. He was nobody's fool, he didn't shout from rage or attempt to get away from me and find his gun. He made no noise or faces or anything, but he caught my foot before I could snatch it back and tried to roll over with it, the way one detaches a leg of fried chicken. I rolled with him and explored his groin with the heel of my other foot. He let go and shied off, got his hands on the floor, and jumped over in a quick somersault.

That was all right. I didn't enjoy wallowing around in the dust myself so much. We were near the kitchen sink, grinning vacuously at each other, bracing ourselves, arms dangling. The radio had Bing Crosby going now, on a song I didn't even recognize, very soothing and dripping with baritone butterscotch. I wondered what had happened to the gun, and what the ladies were up to. They didn't make a sound, and I couldn't afford a glance over my shoulder.

"Now then, m'boy," I suggested comfortably, watching his eyes. "Let's take it easy, huh? Let's me and you and the girls all go back to the ranch and talk this over with the Sheriff, kind of civilized-like, what do you say?"

I didn't think he would. There's more future in arguing with a hungry shark than in trying to talk a smart guy into the idea that he can't be smart for twenty-four hours every day. He had too much to lose, anyway. He suddenly grabbed a handful of my shirt, pulled on it, and swung his arm up around my neck, trying for a half nelson.

It didn't come off so well, because the shirt ripped and I had my fists working on his belly, eight to the bar, the way one exercises on the heavy bag. He didn't like that. His beautiful coffee-brown tan bleached several shades, and he backed away from me as fast as he could. For a moment I thought I had him cornered there, but he bounced off the wall and rushed me. He was no boxer, but he had thirty pounds on me, and his condition was A-plus. I had to duck a couple of wild haymakers before I could get a wrist hold on one and slam a shoulder under his armpit.

Something went wrong with that. His feet left the floor all right, but he jumped clear over me, twisting around in mid-air, and he landed with both arms around my neck from behind and a knee in my kidneys. Those are crude tactics, but he was as strong as a wild bull in the mating season, and he gave me a nasty crick in the spine before I could kick and elbow myself out of the hold.

From there on in, things got to be a trifle confused. I didn't want any more of his funny wrestling hugs, so I kept the old left jab going click-click-click in his pretty face while we danced around each other in a narrow circle, and on the radio Dinah Shore was crooning, "I'll Walk Alone," and by and by I started feeling better about the whole business, because the old left jab was bothering him nicely. He'd lost a good deal of speed and spirit, he didn't know how to protect himself, he was bleeding from a cut lip and from the nose, and I had no trouble blocking or ducking his windmill swings. At last I got him backed up against the kitchen table, stabbed him with another left or two, and pulled the cork on a right uppercut.

They teach you how to do that sort of thing. There's no special virtue in it. But it takes a lot of practice to make it foolproof, and I'd been a little out of practice lately. The blow hit him an inch or so high, exploding on the left cheekbone. He grunted, closed his eyes wearily, and sagged to his knees. It seemed like a reasonable moment to allow for a quick look at my public. The ladies had been curiously stingy with their favorable comment and applause so far.

They were still on the other side of the room, I saw now, and they hadn't moved much. Suzy was still standing near the door, and Lonny was still sitting on the bed, with the bundle at her feet. She had the gun, that was the trouble, and she wasn't interested in our antics a bit. She kept it steadily pointed at my sweet little helpmate, who was obviously in a terrific quandary, fascinated by the fight, desperately anxious to do something, yet afraid to step out of line and take a probably unnecessary risk.

"Put the fool thing down, you silly little witch!" I yelled. "This guy killed your brother, do you want to—"

"Johnny, *look out!*"

Something bumped on the back of my head with a loud hollow booming noise. It didn't hurt at all—it was just a queer dopey sensation. The booming didn't stop, it continued reverberating in my ears. There was a waterfall connected with it somewhere close by, and a sudden urgent desire to find it and lie down under it and watch the pretty red flowers on the riverbank and the cool cascade's misty white spray.

There was a bed of sharp pointed rocks under my back, and silence all around, and darkness except for a tiny little moon, not much bigger than a pin point in the sky. I didn't mind the rocks so much, but what did seem like a botheration was that someone had seen fit to cut off my head, just above the Adam's apple, because that was still working when I made an otherwise unsuccessful attempt to swallow.

Perhaps it was just as well, I thought. Perhaps I was on a good thing there. If people didn't have heads, they'd never get into trouble; no more worry about anything, never a cold or a sore tooth or any more nonsense.

The little moon was growing up fast now, coming down in a whale of a rush, not a moon but a bright white comet falling from the sky. Everybody knows you can't run away from a comet, so I lay still, watching it, and sure enough it stopped a few feet short, not so big after all but still round and bright and suddenly very steady. Then I heard a girl's voice from somewhere, a sulky, puzzled voice that said, "But don't you see, I thought your husband was trying to trick me, I didn't *believe* him."

"Never mind," said another voice, soberly. "Can you roll off the bed? Maybe if I can get my fingers on those knots. . . ."

I discovered I did still have my head, or what was left of it, a large sticky shapeless carpetbag full of dull brooding pain, but complete with eyes, ears, a nose, and a kind of mouth functioning erratically on the outside. There was also a little matter of being unable to move, because of the yards and yards of clothesline wound tight around my whole body, pinning my arms to my sides.

I blinked a few times to clear the bleary fog around me, and saw that I was on the cabin floor, under the chimney with the kerosene lamp. About three yards away, Mrs. Suzanne Marshall sat on a plain, sturdy old chair against the wall. Loops of clothesline tied her ankles and wrists together, other loops coiled around her waist, the back of the chair, and a strong-looking wall bracket. Miss Lorna Mae Havers was wriggling on the mattress bed, wrapped up like a Christmas package in the rest of the clothesline. Her blue dress was torn to ribbons, her hair was a mess, and she had a collection of angry bruises all over her face, including two enormous black eyes.

The big gray airplane suitcase stood solidly by the bed.

I took a deep, careful breath, fought the daze out of my brains, and flexed body muscle against my bonds. Not a hope. New high-grade heavy-duty clotheslines, uneroded by weather, will support the weight of two men without half trying. Two dozen loops of it will frustrate a wild rhinoceros. I let myself go limp again, pulled in my stomach, and started wriggling myself.

"Johnny! Darling, are you all right?"

She sounded good and worried. I giggled at her.

"Hell, no. Do I look all right? Has he gone?"

"Yes, but he said he'd be back soon."

Another dizzy spell nearly blacked me out again. The tough twine cut deeper into my skin. It was that kind of knot. I relaxed and gingerly ran my tongue over sandpaper lips.

"No can do," I said weakly. "I'm stuck. Can Lonny roll?"

"He tied me up so *mean!*" Lonny complained for herself. "Because I scratched him and I pulled his hair, and he *struck* me, the dirty beast!"

"Serves you right, sis," I said. "You picked him."

"It's all your fault!" She was on the verge of crying now. "If you'd only kept out of my business. . . . He was the only one I could go to, I knew Mother was in love with him, she was going to marry him if Father'd give her a divorce, but he wouldn't, and he was nasty to her, and she had no *money!* So I had it all arranged, and then you have to come in and spoil everything!"

"Ain't that a shame?" I said. "And so you called him to help you, only we were living in his apartment—that must have been

quite a shock Wednesday night when you heard my voice on the phone, huh? But you found him anyway, and he fixed you up O.K., didn't he, hauling all this stuff in here for you so you'd be comfortable, and plotting with you how *he'd* get the dough for you—the only trouble about that was he figured he could use it himself much better."

"But, darling, why would he want to double-cross her like this?" Suzy demanded in confusion. "I don't understand it. If he's the one Mrs. Havers was interested in, he could get much more through her, surely. This way he only succeeded in making her go back to her husband!"

"Yeah. It's not that simple. I think I know why, but we'll see. He's a character, he is. Know anything about him, Lonny?"

"He was in the m-movies," said the kid, her voice almost breaking on a sob.

I wondered what he'd gone out for. I wondered what he was up to anyway. We were in a jam, but so was he. It would never do for him to leave the three of us tied up here and merrily push off to Mexico with the bag of lettuce. We'd free ourselves somehow in a matter of hours, he'd be picked up in a day or two, he might not even get across the border.

Bob Havers had been the real snag. I could see how he'd meant to swing this originally. Lonny had phoned him at the ranch, and he'd met her somewhere, and he thought he could collect the ransom for her, stick it in a safe deposit, let her go back to Daddy. She was old enough and stubborn enough for him to trust her, she'd hang onto some likely story they'd cook up together, she'd never give him away. Then he could afford to put the bee on Alice: Alice would know, but he could make her shut up about it; and once she did she'd be hooked good as an accomplice after the fact.

But Bob had caught on, had probably followed him, and he was up against it—kill or lose, the whole lovely proposition blown up from under him, jail, disgrace, Alice gone, every penny gone, not a scrap left worth living for. So he'd shot Bob, but then the jigsaw puzzle didn't fit any more. It meant he couldn't afford to trust Lonny or Alice either. He couldn't make them shut up, or make them tell likely stories, or count on any kind of co-operation, the minute they found out about it. He was strictly on his own from there on in. He couldn't even stop and call the whole thing off.

I had a kind of reluctant admiration for his cool nerve and for the amount of low cunning he had exhibited in his calculations. Those carefully timed phone calls, from the Casa Romero bungalow of course, the skillfully disguised voice reading a well-rehearsed script, the glib feint to deflect the police, the clever timing and the smooth advantage taken of his confidential position, of the circumstances that put him practically beyond the merest shadow of suspicion. He'd had atrocious luck, that was all. Bob Havers, Spencer, Alice, the Marshalls, Marescu, Hogan—every one of us on the wrong foot, making mistakes, blundering around, yet somehow banding together to complicate his problems, failing to play our hands the way he meant us to, the way he could reasonably expect. It didn't seem fair.

On the other hand, he had the money, and he had us. The money was marked, but he was probably fully aware of that, and for an unscrupulous and intelligent man who knows his way around there are plenty of methods and places to dispose of hot money. There are, however, not so many methods to dispose of troublesome people. I started wriggling again, trying hard to bend my legs. The predatory twine took a fresh bite on me in many different and inconvenient spots, but I managed somehow to reach an awkward semireclining position with my shoulders against the chimney wall.

The porch creaked under quickly stepping feet, the door was flung open, and he walked in on us, just as jaunty and self-assured as ever, in spite of the angry marks my knuckles had left on his pleasantly handsome features. He was carrying tools under one arm, and he dropped them casually in a corner where they landed with a noisy clang. I felt a sudden and generous supply of ice cubes forming in my stomach. The tools were a farmer's spade and pitchfork, both of them clogged with raw soil.

He saw me struggling, so he walked over and stood looking down at me with that congenital winning smile of his.

"Well, Major, how's the patient?"

"The patient," I said, more or less dispassionately, " is doing as well as can be expected. He could use a drink."

He nodded at me, gravely polite, and produced a silver hip flask and a glass from the kitchen sink, poured me a liberal dose, and held the glass to my lips. The brandy hissed down my desiccated throat and ran like a stream of wildfire through my system, but it cleared the fog and most of the pain out of my head.

"That's better," I said. "Now suppose you continue acting your age and take this silly rope off of us, so we can all be comfortable and discuss this business like people."

He just laughed at me and shook his head no, that wasn't the idea at all. He pumped some

water into the sink, found a piece of soap and a towel, and started washing his hands and his face.

"Now look, Henry," I said persuasively. "You know you can't get anywhere on this. Your best bet is to play this one for courtesy of the table. With a good lawyer you can make a jury believe you had a fight with Bob, and the gun went off by mistake or something. You're young enough to stand a few years in the big house for manslaughter. We might even make a deal with you and agree on a story that'll put some saccharine in this snatch rap, scale it down to extortion, and go easy on the witness stand. There's always a way, you know that."

He finished wiping his hands, lighted a cigarette for himself and another one for each of us. He was the most considerate devil I've ever come across. He leaned against the chimney under the lamp, smoking peacefully, with all three of us staring at him.

"It was a pity about Bob," he said calmly. "Bob never did trust me. I don't know why. He was generally moody and suspicious of most everybody. Then last Monday night he heard the dog barking at me in the bathhouse, and he came down into the garden in his pajamas to call it off, and of course he saw me wearing the Boss's bathrobe, you know. He even noticed the perfume, I'd put so much of it on so Mrs. Marshall would be sure to recognize it."

Suzy gasped, she was so surprised.

"You mean it was *you* who called me out of bed and made me go down there, not Mr. Havers?" she demanded indignantly.

"That's O.K.," I said smoothly. "He wanted to help Alice — they didn't have sufficient evidence, so he thought he'd manufacture some. All he had to do was put a heavy glove on his left hand, hold the arm stiff, wrap a towel around his hair, and stay in the dark. He could imitate the voice easily, he's good at that. Of course, he had no idea what Lonny was up to, or that we'd be quite so much offended as to check out in the middle of the night."

"It was that infernal dog," he confessed ruefully. "I meant to run for a quick change in my own room, and come back to the bungalow, to tell you I'd been walking in the garden and I'd seen what happened. I'd have tried to apologize to you on Mr. Havers' behalf, and I was going to suggest myself that you'd better leave and take my apartment for awhile. But when I finally got there, you were already gone, and I found your note, so I worried how we could ever find you again in time for you to appear in court."

"And in the morning, the minute you heard Lonny was missing, it occurred to you to have the Sheriff help you bring us in, didn't it, professor? Before the wire from Buzz Marshall denouncing us arrived?"

"Yes, that's quite right, Major," he admitted, giving me a quizzical wink. "I had a two-day old stub in an ash tray in my own room, and I remembered how the night before you'd walked off into the garden with yours. It was just a temporary expedient; it wouldn't have hurt you once you were found. I'm a little ashamed of it anyway, it was such a spur-of-the-moment improvisation and quite unnecessary the way things turned out."

"But you must have known all the time!" Suzy interrupted him in exasperation. "Mrs. Havers must have told you—"

"Not until I phoned her around lunchtime on Tuesday," he assured us earnestly.

"Of course," I said. "If you'd known about Lonny in advance, you'd have stopped her and told her not to be a silly little fool, you'd take care of the situation all right. The whole thing was just a lot of bother from your point of view, at that stage. It meant you had to work overtime trying to sort things out, prevent a scandal, and keep everybody happy, especially us. We were the valuable ones, we were your private investment, but we were kind of hard to handle, you discovered. We might not have made such good witnesses as you'd planned

for us to be after all. That's why
you switched horses when Lonny
came to you for help Wednesday
night. From there on in we became a dangerous nuisance. Then
Bob had to interfere, and you
were saddled with a corpse instead."

"He was hiding in the back of
the car, Thursday evening," said
Henry, apologetically. "I drove
up to the cabin, taking some small
stuff, and on the return trip he
sneezed. I almost ran into a tree.
It was such a pity."

"And you intended to dump
him in Marescu's garage, to give
the cops a run for their money,"
I said. "But when you got there,
you saw our car outside, so we
were elected. Maybe the Sheriff
could stop us now. You should
have left the gun in our glove
compartment; that might have
done it."

"I was afraid maybe they could
trace it," he confessed. He took
the big black pistol out of his coat
pocket and looked at it. "Anyway,
I need it now," he added thoughtfully.

We all kept a cold, uneasy silence for several seconds while
that infernal radio gurgled on and
on with a dull routine selection
from *The Merry Widow.*

"Listen, you haven't got any
crazy ideas about killing the whole
bunch of us off like so many flies,
have you?" I managed at last,
making a fair effort to sound rea-

sonable. "You're not nuts or anything, I hope? If you're so all-
fired keen to get your hands on
that dough, go ahead and take it
away. We'll promise to give you
twenty-four hours start. It'll take us
that long at least to free ourselves."

Hs beamed on me, smiling his
sunniest smile.

"Sorry, Major," he said cheerfully. "You know how it is. Twenty-four hours would be no use to
me. I'll have to go back to the
ranch and tell them there was no
message at the filling station, but
you stopped me on the way home,
claiming you had a lead, and you
made me put the money in your
car and ordered me to follow you.
Then you drove north so fast I lost
you somehwere near Santa Bar-
bara, and I had to give up. They-
're bound to believe me, and they-
'll never find you, or Lonny either,
and I'll have all the time I need,
six months or a year, if necessary.
I've already put up your car in a
cave near by. Nobody ever comes
here anyway, this cabin was
abandoned years ago."

He broke the gun to inspect
the load and barrel and clicked it
together again with the casual de-
tachment of a surgeon adjusting
his mask and glancing over his
favorite instruments. There was
nothing of the wild-eyed maniac
about him, no gleeful anticipation, no rancor or anything churl-
ish. He wasn't even in much of a

hurry. The job was distasteful to him, very much so, but he was a hopelessly narcissistic boy, without a trace of moral scruples, determined to have that dough and stay out of the hangman's hands, and satisfied he knew just how to go about it. He took a step or two toward the bed, and Lonny screamed, heaving herself away from him against the wall. It was a scream that rasped through my eardrums, and it made the hackles come away from my collar.

"Don't be a bloody fool, Henry," I snapped, fighting to suppress the croak in my voice. "You'll never bluff Hogan with that story. He'll trip you up before you're half through telling it. He'll check every inch of it. The minute he talks to that filling station manager—"

"But there was no message, Major!" he assured me, turning around. He sounded surprised with me and a little hurt. "Don't you see, it wasn't necessary. I just brought an empty envelope to flash when I came out, because I knew you'd be observing me, and you'd expect me to have one."

He took another step to the bed and thumbed back the Magnum's hammer. The hammer needed a spot of oil—it made a small grating noise. Someone started laughing, not by any means hysterically—a gay, provocative, lilting laugh, the laugh of a pretty and flirtatious girl dallying with an attractive and highly amusing young man over an intimate little dinner for two. It curled my hair and grew baby barnacles on my teeth. My own sweet little bride and self-elected partner in calamity, having ever such a good time.

It shook him up all right. He swung away from the bed to where she sat swaddled in clothesline on the old chair, giving him the merry ha-ha, her wide gray eyes bright and guileful, but with her lovely red lips opening roguishly in an almost sensual challenge.

"Henry, darling, now *really*. . . . We can do better than that, you know we can. Was it really you who kissed me that night by the swimming pool, not Mr. Havers?"

He stared at her, bewildered, a bit shocked, trying to make out what she was up to. He was paying no attention to me, and I'd been struggling with the rope around my legs for quite a while. I felt like it was loosening up. He was some five or six feet away from me, and I was gauging the chances of a quick lunge and a kick behind his knees. It might work, if he fell and happened to knock himself out on the floor, or on the edge of the table.

"Did it ever occur to you I might have liked it, if I had *known*? Listen, I've got a much better idea. I'll give it to you if you'll be nice and let me team up with you. It won't take much time, and there's no risk at all." They were unconvincing words, but her voice sang a sultry siren promise of very interesting possibilities. It was a flattering, wheedling voice, teasing and tickling, catering to the most primitive male vanity. He lowered the gun and let it dangle. He actually forgot to smile.

"But I thought . . . ," he said, hesitating and throwing a puzzled glance at me over his shoulder.

"Oh, we'll fix *him!*" she countered disdainfully. "I've been sick of him for a long time, he's such a stupid bullying prig, and he's never made a penny or done anything clever in all his life. Look, you don't have to take any chances. You can leave some of this rope on me if you like, but let's go outside for a minute where we can talk. I don't want them to hear. . . ."

The scowl on my face would have worried Boris Karloff. It may have helped, because Henry saw it, and he immediately reached with his free hand for the knots that would release her.

Then it happened, so fast it still makes me dizzy to think of it. He had his hand on the ropes, and he was fumbling with them, when a rapid patter of feet sounded on the porch outside. The rickety door of the cabin burst open with a loud crash, and the huge brown bulk of Khan came rocketing in. The big hound caromed off the opposite wall, got its hind legs back under it, saw the girl on the chair, the man reaching for her, and the gun. It didn't stop to ask questions. It opened a pair of jaws wide enough to admit a boiled leg of lamb, uttered a growl that shook the roof, and jumped straight at the man's throat.

Detective Lieutenant David Hogan kept his tough gray features severely impassive and his clear blue eyes stolidly critical.

"I still figure we oughta throw the book at you," he said coldly. "We got laws in this country you folks don't seem to have so much respect for. So O.K., we could maybe learn you not to mess around with police business. Dumb luck, that's all that got you out this time. It ain't right."

It was late Sunday morning, and we were back in our Westwood apartment after many weary hours of hustle and bustle, of endless grilling and interminable routine dramatics. We could do no more than just sit there and grin at him listlessly.

"See my lawyer, Lieutenant," I told him, waving a drowsy hand.

Mr. Earl G. Spencer sat forward on the edge of the couch, fixing him with a bright contentious glare.

"It appears to me conclusively evident that my clients have conducted themselves in a most exemplary and highly meritorious manner," he asserted dryly. "There is no doubt in my mind that they saved Miss Havers' life and that their contribution toward the solution of Fleming's crimes has been substantial. I am inclined to believe that they would have succeeded in achieving these desirable results even without the timely intervention of the dog, who had apparently conceived an affection for Mrs. Marshall and who must have been roaming about the estate for several days in search of her; possibly its attention was attracted by the sound of gunshot during my client's first struggle with Fleming. However that may be, I have been instructed by Mr. and Mrs. Havers to offer the dog as a token of their gratitude to them, together with this check in partial reimbursement for the pains and expense they have suffered in their courageous efforts on Miss Havers' behalf."

He handed me the check, and I summoned up enough energy to blink at the figure on it. Hogan watched me with a cynical groove curving his upper lip, obviously his best attempt at a more or less good-natured leer.

"All I ask is you should lay off or get a license," he said reasonably.

"If my client should wish to establish himself in this county as a private investigator," said Spencer, spoiling his own dignity with a twinkle, "I shall in due course place an application for his license as such before the proper authorities."

The little woman and I looked at each other, keeping our faces straight without too much difficulty. She reached out to fondle the grim brown head that filled her lap.

"Khan, honey, you all reckon we ought to go and make us legal?" she inquired sweetly of her new hero.

The great Dane opened one moist, reluctant eye, closed it again, and yawned, not bothering to move its muzzle. It was a small, courteous yawn that betrayed itself only by a tiny belching whine.

LOOK FOR THE NEXT BESTSELLER MYSTERY—OUT NOV. 17

On the site where the dwellings of an ancient tribe had recently been uncovered, a corpse was discovered. But this corpse was no relic of the past—in fact, it had been very much alive the day before. . .

SPOOKED MURDER

by MANVILLE CHAPMAN

PIKE RIGGS HAD BEEN CHASING a ghost when he dropped into blackness. He dropped by stepping into a four-foot hole in the uneven surface of a mesa top. The walls of the hole slanted sharply away and Pike had been in free fall perhaps twenty feet, his long arms and legs spread-eagled as they plunged into sandy bottom. He pulled himself gingerly to his knees, looked up at the oval of night sky, and then wondered how that white-clad figure he had been chasing had known enough to dodge around such a hole. Maybe it really had been a ghost, the kind that could tread on thin air.

Pike felt cautiously around and his hand encountered cloth. Then he remembered the small electric flashlight he always carried like a pen; he pulled it out, jabbed the switch button, and discovered he was kneeling beside a prone figure —a man with his head bashed in.

Pike stared at the dead man and knew instantly that this was no accidental death, at least not from a fall. There were no jutting rocks against which a falling body would smash, and the floor of the hole was all sand. His own fall had been without difficulty. Pike had seen enough corpses in the war to recognize what looked like a head bashed in with some blunt instrument. Pike had dropped in on a murder and that was what he deserved for chasing a ghost.

Of course, everyone back at the Turtle Creek Guest Ranch had attempted to discourage Pike Riggs' visiting Hua-pe ruins that evening. They were a group of recently uncovered dwellings of an ancient tribe on the Parajito Plateau that extended back from the Turtle Creek Valley.

Carey Breen, an archaeologist, had been enthused over his recent discovery of some pictographs during the course of the excavation

103

work. Discussing pictographs around Pike Riggs was certain to bring action. Pike was a curio peddler, a collector and trader of Indian blankets and silver. But no modern trinkets could interest him more than the prehistoric. He brought his lithe six feet up from a couch in the ranch house living room and demanded of Carey Breen, "Let's go see your pictographs, then!"

"Now? It's dark!"

"We can take flashlights."

Carey Breen's pale blue eyes behind thick-lensed glasses looked very dubious. "I dig around Hua-pe daytime without thought of trouble. But at night it's weird—"

Pike snorted. "You're spooked!"

Carey shrugged his chunky shoulders. He was shoulder high to Pike, but he was stocky and looked able to take care of himself with any spooky adversary.

"Don't believe in ghosts. But I did see some kind of white figure up on the mesa one night, and along with what the Jemez Indians say—"

Carey stopped. At that moment, Pablo Kayenta, the Jemez Indian who worked around the ranch as a handy man and guide, came in with a log for the fireplace. He went stolidly about his work.

Carey looked uneasily at Pablo and then went on explaining to Pike, "You should understand this, with your curio trader background. The Pueblos all say there is a curse on the man who probes around the dwellings of their ancestors by night and disturbs their long sleep."

Pike smiled. "Maybe some of the old men in the clans feel this way." He looked at Pablo thoughtfully. The Jemez had been educated in government schools he knew, and like so many others, when he had returned to his Pueblo he had reverted back to tribal custom. He was dressed in a G-string and breech cloth, and his brown legs glistened in the moonlight above yellow moccasins. His hair had the square Pueblo cut in bangs.

He addressed the Pueblo Indian softly, "Ai-he, Pablo. The spirits of the mesa dwellers come back to haunt Hua-pe?"

Pablo straightened from his task to stare intently at Pike. "The trader knows the mesa dwellers have long ago gone back to Shipapu to live eternally. Why should their spirits return to piles of rocks?"

Pike nodded. "Then what is this white figure that runs over Hua-pe ruins by night?"

"There are springs on the edge of the mesa and my people say the Ah-won-yah are there to guard the water. Who can say what the white men have seen? But the Ah-won-yah are there to see that no one harms the springs." Pablo turned swiftly and left the room on silent moccasins.

Pike Riggs turned to smile sardonically at Carey Breen. "No fret there, as long as you don't dynamite the springs. But look, Carey, you don't need to bother. Nat Towndrow will probably show me the way."

"Well, if you like, Pike. But better still, wait for morning, huh?"

But Pike couldn't seem to find Nat Towndrow, the other archeologist who stayed at the guest ranch while they were carrying on their work. He looked for the owner of the ranch, Hank Stowe, and then finally found Hank's pretty wife, Marion, as she gathered up some extra bedding from one of the cabins.

"Lord, Pike, I don't know where either of those scamps have gone. Hank may be taking a nap some place so he'll be good and ready to stay up all hours like he usually does." She laughed and then her voice took a more serious turn. "But Nat isn't in his cabin or any place. I looked for him after dinner and he said he'd be around."

Pike speculated at the concern in her voice. When he had been a law student a Ann Arbor, Marion had also been a student at the University of Michigan, and so had Nat Towndrow. Pike had decided law was not for him and had left before Nat Towndrow's romance with Marion had developed and then broken off. But he had heard about it. Marion was a

startling brunette and Nat was a nordic blonde and they had been handsome together. But years later, Pike had found Marion married to Hank Stowe and living in his own Southwest. And then Nat Towndrow had come along later with Carey Breen to work on Huape ruins and naturally they had come to live at Hank Stowe's Rancho because it was a guest place and close to their work. But it left Pike wondering at times.

"Well, I had a wild notion that I wanted to see those pictographs of Carey's by moonlight and I thought Nat or Hank would guide me up to the Mesa. Carey doesn't much want to go."

Marion laughed. "Carey thinks the ruins are haunted. Well, I'd take you, Pike, but I'm behind in some of this everlasting work." She darted a sudden glance at Pike. "Maybe Carey is right. It might be dangerous."

"Bosh. I'm like a cat. I can see in the dark. Think I'll find the rock scrapings on my own."

"Well, here. You'd better take a big flashlight, just in case your cat lamps get fogged."

The white beam from the electric torch carried by Pike went poking like a finger around the crumbling walls of Hua-pe. Some of the ancient dwellings still lay half buried leaning against a sheer cliff that was dotted with rows of forbidding caves. A wind was shrilling past the openings but even so the silence of ages pressed down all around.

Pike's light showed an exposed circular room that had been subterranean. It was now roofless and about thirty feet in diameter. This was the Kiva, or lodge room, that Carey and Nat had excavated in the months past. Carey had told him that the pictographs had been uncovered up a trail beyond this point, almost on the edge of the mesa.

Pike started climbing. Almost at the top of the trail he stopped for a moment to catch his breath and then on the mesa edge he saw in the sudden light of a rising moon a figure in white darting past a crevice in the rocks!

Pike started after it without hesitation. Pictographs could wait. Here was action. He left the trail and started at a wild run along the cliff edge where it was smooth going. Then the white figure ran down below the rim of what appeared to be a small canyon. It turned out to be a coulee three or four feet below the mesa floor.

Pike's light stabbed the breadth of it, but the white figure had followed some trail out. He went quickly along the rim to spot an opening between boulders where he could jump to the level below. He went too quickly and his light was concentrated too much on the coulee instead of the rim.

He stepped into a depression. Next he was slipping. He threw his flashlight and tried to grab rock with both hands but there was nothing to hold on to. He went through a hole that was like the bottom of a shallow funnel and next he was falling downward.

Eventually, he recovered his senses and his pocket flashlight showed him he was kneeling by a corpse. He rose to his feet so as to get a look at the dead man's face. It was Nat Towndrow, Carey Breen's co-worker and friend.

Marks in the sand told him that Nat Towndrow had been dragged into this place. He hadn't been dropped from above. Moreover, the tracks to either side of the dragged trail showed him moccasin prints and they came from a tunnel in the wall of the conical-shaped cave.

An archeologist friend in Santa Fe had told Pike the prehistoric *kivas* sometimes had openings beside the entrance way. If his sense of direction was correct that tunnel led to the kiva that had been excavated by Nat Towndrow. He stepped close to the tunnel mouth and felt the draft of cold air and knew he was right.

But before leaving he had to take one precaution. Quickly he went back to Nat Towndrow's body and searched his pockets. There was a knife, a coin purse, and a billfold with a note in it. He pocketed the other things but spread out the note to read it beneath his flashlight. It was type-written carefully:

"Nat
Meet me at the Kiva shaft soon after dinner. I may be delayed—so wait.
K."

Pike slowly folded the note and returned it to his pocket with the other things. The K stood for Kayenta possibly. Pablo Kayento could probably type since he had been in a government school. His eyes darted back to the moccasin tracks in the sand. There was always the Pueblo Indian antagonism to white men digging around in the buried homes of the ancients. Pablo Kayenta had been raised in an Indian Pueblo and his years of civilized schooling might not alter entrenched tribal beliefs.

Pike's thoughts went skittering as he felt gravel fall about him. Quickly he turned off his flash-light and looked up at the oval hole. He was certain he saw the shape of shoulders and head pulled back from the opening.

Without using the flashlight again he felt his way to the tunnel and stooped to go through its length. It was short and direct. Soon he saw the moon-bathed kiva floor a few feet below the tunnel entrance. But before emerging, Pike surveyed the area before him.

And his caution was rewarded. A white shape came slowly across the trampled kiva floor. It came close to the tunnel entrance and

Pike laughed sardonically to him-self. This was the ghost and it was nothing more than Marion Stowe in a white Chimayo woven coat with a round hood that came up over her dark hair.

Pike stepped out of the tunnel and Marion drew back with appar-ent fright. Then she said quickly, "Pike! I've been wondering what happened to you. Did you find the pictographs?"

"Not quite. Found a cave that interests me though."

"Shouldn't think you'd want to be exploring caves at night."

Pike laughed. "Just as easy as in daytime. They're dark."

"Well—I can show you the pic-tographs now that I'm here. I came up wondering if you were lost."

So Pike walked beside her and they started climbing the trail out of the kiva. They carried on a spasmodic conversation while Pike's mind really worked on time elements. He had seen head and shoulders at the hole in the roof of the kiva shaft just a few mo-ments before emerging from the tunnel and meeting Marion. So, obviously those hadn't been her shoulders twenty feet or so up on the mesa top. His eyes watched closely the rim of the mesa but he saw no moving thing. All was eerie moonlight and silence except for their own scuffing, climbing footfalls.

Near the top of the trail, Marion turned along the rim and they came to the pictographs. They were carvings in a lava cliff. Gray dust-filled lines in the dark surface told a story with symbols as old as man: the tiny round shape open at one end denoting a spring; the parallel wavy lines of a river coming from the spring; and over all, the semi-circle cross hatched to show night with circles centered by dots to show the great spirits above all this. Here was Ah-won-yah guarding the water supply of all living things.

Pike smiled slightly and turned to Marion. "This is what the Jemez Indians believe—that Ah-won-yah guards the rim of the mesa, from which the springs that feed the stream below come. And before I came to the pictographs tonight, I saw a white shape darting over the rimrock."

Marion looked at Pike curiously, "You believe in the Indian spirits, Pike?"

"I like the stories about them. Belief is seeing." He reached forward and touched the sleeve of her white Chimayo coat. "But then I could have seen a white coat like this one."

Marion laughed nervously. "You think I might have been up on the rimrock earlier, Pike?"

"Were you?"

Marion Stowe's dark eyes searched Pike's impassive face. But she never answered. Instead there came an interruption from far down in the valley. A flash of light near the roadside and then moments later the sound of an explosion. Then a fire raged at the edge of some cottonwood trees.

Pike exclaimed, "That sounded like a gas tank explosion. Maybe a car is on fire down there."

Marion had already started down the trail. "Come on! We must tell them at the ranch house."

They didn't reach the ranch house. A car was coming through the gateway, driven by Hank Stowe. He skidded to a stop when he saw Pike and Marion. "Hop aboard. There's a fire down the road. The cook says Carey and Pablo have already gone down there."

Marion asked quickly, "Have you seen Nat, Hank?"

"No, can't say that I have. Of course he might have been with Carey and Pablo. The cook didn't say so."

Pike knew the answer to that one. Well, after the fire was over, he would get them all together and they'd go up the trail again to look at Nat Towndrow's body laid out in a cave. But he'd have to watch his step. He remembered the head and shoulders of someone looking through the kiva shaft while he bent over Nat Towndrow's body. That person might not want him divulging the evidence of a murder just yet.

Hank came to a fast braked stop near the fire and Pike's guess proved to be right. It was a station wagon burning from front to rear. Carey Breen and Pablo Kayenta were running with buckets of water from the stream, trying to douse the flames. Pike and Hank Stowe ran to help them. But the station wagon was charred ruins moments later. The heat subsided some after a while, and they could determine that there was a body on the seat of the car. There had to be, because the car had been driven by someone off a sharp road bend into a telephone line.

Finally they managed to get the charred remains of the driver out of the car and to the ground. It was Marion Stowe who saw the ring on what had once been a finger. "Nat Towndrow!" She barely breathed the name. "Nat had a signet ring like that one!"

Hank Stowe went over to put a big arm around his wife. "Steady, gal. This is rough. I didn't have any idea, or I wouldn't have let you come down here."

Pike was watching the huge, good natured rancher. He decided to hazard a question, "Hank, did you hear the sound of the explosion?"

Hank Stowe looked around at Pike. "Nope. Can't say that I did. I was takin' me a snooze when the cook came pounding at my door and said there was a fire up the road."

Pike looked at Carey and the archeologist answered without question, "Yes, I heard it. Pablo and I ran for my car about the same time. We could see the flames down the road from the ranch."

So that was that. Pike knew only one thing. Nat Towndrow had never driven that car off the road. That he had been placed in it, after being carried away from the cave up on the hillside was entirely possible. And whoever had carried out that task could also have driven the car into the telephone pole, set it afire, and make his way back to the ranch. The explosion would have come when the flames reached the gas tank.

Later, Hank Stowe tried to phone the Deputy Sheriff at Bernallilo but the line was dead. Hank said in a tired voice, "I was afraid of that. Nat's car hit that telephone pole and broke the line. It's a long drive to go in and tell them. But I can do what I did when the storm broke down the wires last month. I'll drive over the mesa where that lookout cabin is located. There's a private phone there, and they left a key to the place with me." He turned to the other men, "Any you fellers like to go with me?"

Pike declined quickly. "I have a letter to write. I'll borrow your typewriter if I may, Marion?"

Marion nodded as Carey Breen announced, "I'm going to bed for the second time. But I probably won't sleep after seeing Nat that way."

But Pablo Kayenta was not so dispirited. "I'm hungry." He started for the kitchen.

Marion made a face of distaste. "Pablo, to eat after that!"

The Pueblo Indian remarked impassively, "I work pretty hard since supper."

Pike glanced quickly at the Pueblo, "You mean since dinner, don't you, Pablo?"

"Nope, mean supper." And he departed.

After the others had left, Pike snooped around in the little office off the living room. He opened the portable typewriter and found a half sheet of paper set in the carriage. Some thrifty soul had used a half sheet and preserved the rest for future use. He brought out the note he had taken from Nat Towndrow's pocket, unfolded it and fitted it to the half sheet. It matched.

He folded the two pieces together to return them to his pocket and then he noticed the initials on the portable typewriter case. M.K.S. Marion K. Stowe, probably. That initial K again. He decided to talk with the lady of the house.

Marion was coming from the kitchen on her way to the living room. Pike showed her the note without preamble. She colored as she glanced at it. She nodded. "Yes, I wrote it. My middle name is Kay and Nat used to call me that sometimes. I was going to tell you that I was up on the mesa rim earlier to meet him. He didn't make it, and I came back. Then when you left to see the pictographs I went up by the back trail to suggest that he had better leave before you met him. I thought it might be embarrassing."

"So that white coat of yours started the story about the ghost."

Marion nodded. "Nat and I didn't know how to set Carey straight without admitting our rendezvous on the mesa." She was talking now with her eyes staring straight ahead of her. "You remember, Pike, that Nat and I were sweethearts in College. I didn't mean to have it start all over again but I guess it did. But now it is over." She looked back at Pike with a sudden realization, "But the note? Nat must have had it with him! How on earth do you happen to have it now?"

Pike took a deep breath. "I found it in the bottom of the kiva ventilation shaft up at Hua-pe ruins—on Nat Towndrow's dead body."

"On Nat's body!" She sank into a pigskin chair, her face white. "Then he was dead before the accident. He wasn't killed in his car?"

"He was murdered—probably up near Hua-pe."

Marion shrank back and her lips soundlessly formed the dread word, "Murdered!" Terror came into her eyes.

But Pike had to ask the question that had been in his mind. "About these meetings with Nat. Did Hank know anything about them?"

Marion came out of the chair and caught Pike's arm in a hysterical grip with trembling hands. "Pike, no! I know what you are thinking; but it isn't so. Hank is too kind to kill anyone. And he always just laughed at my flirtations with his friends at parties and dances. He hasn't a jealous bone in his body." She paced away excitedly from Pike and then swung on him again. "Why, Nat was the jealous one. He became furious last Christmas when Carey Breen gave me my Chimayo coat as a gift."

"Oh. So Carey is an admirer also?"

Marion made a deprecatory gesture. "Oh you know, Pike. All my life men have been attentive to me. These things like gifts and flirtations mean nothing serious." She stopped short and stared at him. "Oh, you big lunk, how would you ever understand all this?"

Pike grinned. "I'm a bachelor. Don't know."

When Pike entered his cabin a few moments later his first surprise was finding the light on, and then he understood why, because his second surprise was a penciled note propped against his pillow. It read:

"Trading in curios is healthier. Why don't you stick to it instead of playing detective? You'd better follow me up to the ranger station and talk over a deal with me.

Hank"

Pike smiled sardonically. As a trader there was nothing he liked better than a deal if he was the dealer. He went back to the kitchen where Pablo Kayenta was finishing his midnight meal.

Pike asked, "Has Hank Stowe a gun?"

Pablo's eyes swept to a gun rack by the kitchen door. "Two rifles there, Trader."

"The two rifles I see. I mean, a hand gun, a pistol, maybe?"

The Pueblo Indian nodded once. "In his car he has one." Then Pablo's face lighted with the apparent memory of something that amused him very much. "The boss he never wants to hurt, so—" Pablo fell into the use of sign language he knew Pike must know. He made the sign for "shoot" with his right-hand fingers pressed against the ball of the thumb and then moving the hand rapidly while snapping the fingers against the thumb, and then he changed the hand to show the index and second fingers spiraling upward from his forehead to indicate "medicine" or "mystery."

Pike laughed. "I thought so. Listen Pablo, you come with me. You have a white sheet like the Taos wear?"

Pablo nodded. Pike said, "Bring it. I will get my station wagon."

Perhaps twenty minutes later, Pike's station wagon pulled up the last steep grade of hill road that had wound over the Pajarito mesa and to the rim on the far side from the Hua-pe ruins. It was here that Pablo Kayenta got out and disappeared into the mesquite.

Pike parked his car at the end of the road beside the battered Stowe car. He noticed in the moonlight that some other car tracks led on into the timber below and he nodded. Without hesitation, he walked over to the ranger station that stood back only a few feet from the rim of the mesa.

There was a light on in the station and the door was open so that the light flooded out on a crumpled figure at the very edge of the cliff. Pike calmly walked over and felt the man's pulse. He was alive. He had been hit over the head but he was tough.

From the side of the cabin came a cold voice. "I figured the note would fetch you, Riggs."

Pike turned and looked into the shadows of the cabin side. He saw dimly the dark figure of the speaker, whose hand was protruding in the moonlight, holding a gun.

"You aim," said Pike slowly, "to shoot me, let me topple off the rim, push the gun in this man's hand and then push him off too. Then when we are found it will look like we had a ruckus up here and fell off the cliff together."

The other asked cautiously, "If you knew it was a trap, why did you come?"

"To see if I could spring the trap."

"Well, this is a loaded gun and my finger's on the trigger. But I'll take a moment to find out when you suspected me!"

"When Marion gave me a clue to the jealousy motive. First you had a fight with Nat Towndrow over Marion. You bashed him in and then hid the body in that kiva shaft. When I stumbled on it, you went in there later while I was with Marion at the pictograph rock. You carried away the body and staged that car accident. Marion figured in this a lot. It had to be jealousy."

"So you didn't fall for the bit about Pablo Kayenta being resentful of archeologists working at Hua-pe."

Pike laughed. "If that Jemez Indian had sent a note to Nat Towndrow to meet him on the mesa he would have called it 'after supper' instead of 'dinner.' And anyway you weren't spooked by a ghost. You only wanted to keep me away from Hua-pe this evening, especially since you'd left Nat Towndrow dead up there."

Carey Breen stepped out of the shadow. "Anyway, they all think you suspected Hank Stowe of the murder of Nat Towndrow over his wife. Now it will look like you accused him and you'll die together. Well, this is it, Riggs. You know too much!"

But he didn't fire immediately. Instead, his eyes opened wide behind their thick-lensed glasses as he looked beyond Pike to the mesa rim. Pike turned and also saw the white figure coming up over the rim, rising out of space apparently.

Carey shouted, "What is this? There's nothing to this story about ghosts. Just a gag. This will show you—" He took careful aim and fired at the approaching white figure, now hardly ten paces away.

The white figure came on. He fired again and stumbled backward. He screamed, "The bullets —they don't stop that thing! What is it?" He turned and ran and then turned to fire once more, still backing away.

Suddenly Carey's footing was bad on the rim edge. He slid sideways and lost his balance. Pike darted forward and tried to reach him, disregarding the menacing gun.

But Carey Breen slid down a steep slope and went over the rim edge screaming. Pike peered downward holding to a cedar at the edge of the mesa rim. He could see a shape lodged in some boulders below. He turned back to look into the face of Pablo Kayenta as the Indian lowered the white sheet that had been swathed around him Taos Pueblo fashion.

Pike said, "He didn't take much stock in spooks—until he found that bullets wouldn't stop your masquerade. That jarred him."

"The bullets," Pablo said, "were the only ghosts." Again the Indian made the signs he had shown Pike down at the ranch house. "Mystery bullets. Blank cartridges in the only gun on the ranch because the boss he say he don't ever want to hurt anybody."

Pike nodded and walked swiftly to the crumpled form of Hank Stowe. "And he hasn't, Pablo. He hasn't hurt anyone and I doubt if he's been hurt too bad himself. We'll get him to the doctor and pick up Carey Breen on the way. Likely he's a dead man after that fall."

Pablo Kayenta looked calmly out over the mesa. "Those men dig for trouble at Hua-pe."

"In more **ways than one,**" amended Pike.

FALL HOUSECLEANING
—a bonanza for mystery lovers!
While they last — 10 books for $1.00

The warehouse at Concord, N. H., is bursting at the seams, and these books *must* go to make room for new stock.

That's why you can now get—while they last—ten (10) different copies of Mercury, Bestseller, and Jonathan Mysteries for only $1.00. They are all in good, readable condition, though we cannot let you choose titles. Send your dollar (or more) to-day to:—

BONANZA

Mercury Press, Inc.

P. O. Box 271

Rockville Centre, N. Y.

The unveiling of Crowther's masterpiece was being hungrily await-
ed by a throng of admirers. Yet, at a time when Crowther should
have been reveling in his new achievement, his only thoughts were
of escape . . .

PERSONAL APPEARANCE

by ROBERT L. FISH

ALL HOLLYWOOD WAS ANX-
iously awaiting the unveiling of
the latest Crowther masterpiece.
The famous display platform on
top of the three-story Crowther
Building at Hollywood and Vine
was enclosed by the usual tarpaulins, but the faint sound of
hammering drifted down from the
roof to the mounting group of bystanders patiently looking up from
the pavement.

The secrecy with which James
Crowther surrounded his displays
prior to their official disclosure
was part of the man's superior
showmanship. His associates, from
draftsman to carpenter, were as
reticent as the great man himself;
partly because they enjoyed the
feeling of participating in the mystery, and also because it would
have meant the jobs of the entire
crew were a design to become pre-
viously known.

But it was not the secrecy alone
that kept the newspapers and

magazines and their readers excited at the thought of a new
Crowther creation. The man was
undoubtedly a genius at his work.
His tableau for the motion picture
Seascape had certainly been simple enough: a gaunt slice of a
three-masted ship, with two sea-
men struggling with the wheel
against a bleak background of
ropes, sea, and clouds. Yet the
crowds that had stormed Hollywood and Vine to watch that
scene had felt the tenseness and
drama of the contest between man
and the elements; and there was
little doubt that the effectiveness
of the Crowther display helped
make that picture the huge success it became.

This latest effort was to exploit
the picture *Dick Turpin,* a Hollywood romance covering the more
glamorous features in the life of
the notorious highwayman. For
three weeks the publicity department of the studio had bombard-

ed the city with advertisements imploring the public to watch for the Crowther display; huge sheets had been prepared consisting solely of a black question mark against a stark splotchy crimson background, with "Watch Crowther" printed beneath. These could be seen on every available wall, and smaller leaflets of the same design had been scattered from airplanes, and stuffed into mailboxes. The campaign had been effective; now, on the evening of the long-heralded premier, curiosity was at a fever pitch, and heavy crowds were gathering to wait for the spotlights to blaze, and the tarpaulins to open.

In his office one flight below the enclosed roof, James Crowther stared across his desk at the famous actor seated there. The desk-lamp provided the only illumination, and under its cruel examination the face of the actor had lost its youth; the curly hair showed streaks of grey. The fullness of the handsome face, without the disguise of make-up, now looked merely gross, the heavy lips petulant. The actor leaned indolently back in the leather chair, idly playing with a pencil on the desk.

"One would almost think," he was saying, "that you were the star of the picture, instead of me. The publicity seems more directed to bringing attention to you and your exhibit, than to me or the picture. Naturally, under those circumstances, I felt it necessary to be sure that the display gives me sufficient personal publicity."

Crowther snorted. "I think you are wasting your time and mine. I am sure that you are familiar with the fact that until midnight tonight, nobody knows the details of the tableau. I am also sure that you know that my contract with the studio gives me complete control over the design."

The actor smiled negligently, his fingers continuing to play with the pencil. "I am familiar with a number of facts," he admitted. "To be honest with you, my present position in pictures is not due so much to my acting ability as to my knowledge of facts. Certain facts. About certain people."

Crowther, who had started to rise, sank back into his chair and frowned across the desk. "I have heard rumors," he finally said quietly, "but I scarcely expected a personal confirmation. Nor do I see why it should have any influence on me or my work."

The actor's smile widened. "Possibly I can clarify the position. You see, among the facts that I happen to possess are certain ones regarding you. Before you became the genius of Hollywood. Before, as a matter of fact, you even became James Crowther!"

In the silence that followed, the great designer waited tensely. After a suitable pause for effect, the actor continued in a soft voice. "Your talents, for example, were less graciously received in England, I believe. Possibly because you used them to duplicate Her Majesty's countenance in competition with the Minories. But as I recall, they failed to call it genius; they called it counterfeiting. Let me see; was it ten years they awarded you with? Or five?" He added apologetically. "I have such a poor memory for sordid details."

Crowther clasped his trembling hands and stared at the sardonic face across from him. "What do you want?" he demanded urgently.

"I have just told you. Simply to see the design and be certain that I receive enough personal publicity in your presentation. Just a favor." The actor looked up from the pencil and met Crowther's frightened eyes squarely. "For the present, just a favor." For a moment the glances of the two men held. Then the designer's eyes fell; he shrugged his shoulders in weary defeat and arose from the desk. "The sketch is here on my drawing board," he said in a shaking voice, turning to the drafting instruments behind him. "I hope you find it satisfactory."

James Crowther closed the door of the cab and leaning forward, tapped the driver on the arm. "International Airport, please."

The cab driver turned his attention from the crowd to his passenger. "Look, Mac," he said eagerly; "Would you mind waiting just a minute? Just a minute, honest. They're going to flash that new Crowther job, midnight sharp, and I'd like to get a gander." Then he thrust his head out of the window and stared up at the building roof.

The designer also put his face to the window and watched. Suddenly spotlights stabbed the night, lighting the roof top. The great canvas curtains swayed a bit in the night wind, and then, driven by hidden motors, gracefully folded to one side. A gasp swept the huge throng gathered in the street.

Against a dark jumbled forest of gnarled, tortured trees, a gigantic scaffold stood, the bare frame and rigid cross-arm gaunt and frightening in the unblinking stare of the spotlights. From the rope's end, a masked, black-garbed figure dangled limply, the arms and legs tightly bound with cord. A shudder rippled over the gaping onlookers, gazing intently at the macabre body twisting against the black night sky.

The cab driver shook his head in wondering admiration, and leaning forward, released the hand brake. "That guy is a genius," he said over his shoulder. "A realist, that's what he is. I've seen every one of his things, and while they're all good, you understand, this is the best. This is the best yet.

"By far," said his passenger sadly, and leaned back in the seat.

He tried to remember Corinne as she used to look. But the only image that kept recurring was of the bullet piercing her skull and abruptly ending her life . . .

DUET

by NORMAN DANIELS

JEFF BARON PICKED up a newspaper from the stand in the lobby of his office building and realized that being found not guilty of murder by a jury doesn't mean the general public goes along with the acquittal.

Molly, the pudgy, thick-fingered woman with the dirty nails, could have refused his money in a polite way. He'd certainly given her a great deal of business in the past. She could have just pushed the dime back at him, instead of spitting on it before she leaned over the counter and dropped it at his feet.

He didn't even look at the newspaper, though he knew his picture was on the front page. He walked toward the bank of elevators. Tommy, the skinny-faced starter, saw him coming and promptly signaled so that the only car on the floor closed its doors and went on up—empty. Jeff would have to wait for another. He remembered giving Tommy

twenty dollars last Christmas. It didn't pay, he told himself. Not with any of these people who exercised petty tyranny.

He walked into his office. It looked strange, like a place he'd seen in his dreams, but doubted was real. It had been eight and a half months since they locked him up. There was a new receptionist and new stenographers and clerks. They all looked up as he entered, but nobody spoke, nobody stopped him. Practically every desk had a copy of the latest edition newspaper on it.

They'd left his name on the office door, at any rate. It read Jeff Baron, President. Inside, a few changes were in the process of being made. Bob Shannon, whom Jeff had groomed for a good job one of these days, was busy packing the books from the wall shelves into large cases. Frank Rossiter sat behind Jeff's desk, idly fingering a metal envelope slitter. He didn't get up.

Frank was hefty, bald, loose limbed and heavy jowled. "Hello, Jeff," he said. "I'm glad they let you go."

"Thanks. Jeff looked around the office. "Hello, Bob."

Bob nodded, kept on working. Jeff faced Frank again. "What's going on?" he asked.

"I'm going to be as blunt as I have to be, Jeff," Frank said. "It may hurt, but this cannot be helped. Your father began this book publishing business and you took it over at his death. We publish religious and school text books. We can't afford to have a man of your repute associated with such a delicate operation, so the board has voted unanimously to replace you. We own sufficient stock to do it. However, you will receive an income based upon your share holdings, so you certainly have no complaints. That's all. If you'll excuse me. . . ."

He got up and moved ponderously toward the door. Jeff watched him for a moment.

"I thought the foreman of the jury said, 'Not Guilty,' Frank."

Frank didn't look around. He did close the door noisily and hard. Bob threw a handful of books into the case he was packing. He was a handsome young man, dependable, and he'd always been loyal. If it hadn't been for Jeff, he'd still be down in the shipping room pasting labels on packages.

"He didn't have to do it that way," Bob said.

Jeff sat down at his desk and pulled open the drawers. They hadn't been touched since the police ransacked them and they were in a sorry state.

"I've never thanked you for coming to see me," he said, without looking up. "You're the only one in the organization who did."

"Yes," Bob said. "I figured you were getting a raw deal. I'd have sworn you were, Mr. Baron."

"You would have sworn . . . ?"

"Yes, sir. You told the cops, the jury, everybody, that you hadn't taken Corinne out at any time and you had no reason to kill her. Corinne's sister said you took her out plenty, but I didn't believe her. Not until . . ." He took the envelope from his pocket and dropped it on the desk. The snapshots spilled out before Jeff. The snaps he knew Corinne had taken and the existence of which he dreaded.

"I found them in one of the books, just this morning," Bob said. "I'm glad it wasn't before the jury gave its verdict, because I wouldn't have known what to do with them. You gave me this job . . . I always respected you . . ."

"Thanks," Jeff said. "Whatever I did for you, has been amply repaid."

Bob went to the door. "I'll finish up after you leave, sir. The stuff will be shipped to your house tomorrow."

Jeff nodded. You too, he thought. My last hope for friendship. All because of an indiscretion he was swept into so fast, he hardly realized it had happened. He pulled a large ash tray over, set fire to the snaps one by one and watched them burn. Corinne in a bathing suit was an attractive sight to behold. Remembering her brought it all back. Just two days —that's all it had been, at this well-hidden lake resort. Two days, and it had cost Corinne her life. He angrily wished the flames would consume the photos faster.

It didn't take long to clean out his desk. He packed everything in an old brief case he'd stowed away in the supply closet years ago. He took one final look at the office, where he'd practically grown up. The wall behind the great desk, where his father's lifesize oil had been hung, was faded. They didn't have to take that down, he thought.

He walked through the main office. Nobody looked up. He took the elevator down. The operator had worked there for twenty years and had known his father. He stared straight ahead. Jeff didn't embarrass him by any greeting.

The wide, stately-looking house in which he'd been born looked wonderful as the cab rolled up the curved drive to the front door. He was glad that he'd phoned Lydia not to meet him at the courthouse. If she'd ever gone through what had just happened to him. . . .

Lydia stood waiting at the top of the porch steps while he paid the driver. When he took her in his arms, it was tenderly, and with all the love the months in jail had stored up within him. She was no glamour-puss, this woman he'd married twenty odd years ago. But she was capable and she was proud. She knew how to wear clothes, patronized the best hairdressers and she was interesting to be with.

"It's nice to be home," he said.

She was shorter than he by four inches, but that didn't make her any midget, for he was over six feet tall. Her eyes were a cool, calm grey.

"I know what must have happened at the office. Was it bad, darling?"

She didn't know all. She had no idea about the snapshots. He shuddered inwardly at the thought.

"I more or less expected it, Lydia. Shall we go in?"

Nothing had changed in the house. There were fresh flowers everywhere, which meant the garden and the little greenhouse had done well. He walked into the spacious and rich-looking living room. Lydia caught up with him.

"Jeff," she said, "we might as well get all the bad things said and done with. Stan has left school. He isn't coming home. He says he thinks you're guilty. He entered law school last fall, you remember. They used your case—all the evidence—to conduct mock trials. Stan . . . just left. He's in the city looking for a job."

Jeff wasn't even hurt. When Stan had never once paid him a visit or showed up at the trial, he sensed the boy's conviction of his father's guilt. Stan had never been his son anyway. Not the way he'd been Lydia's.

"I'm sorry he feels that way," Jeff said. He took her by the shoulders, gently and carefully, and turned her to face him. "You, Lydia? How do you feel about me? Is it just loyalty that keeps you here?"

"Jeff, did you murder Corinne?"

"No!"

She stood on tiptoe and kissed him. "Then there is nothing more to say. I've made a special dinner. We let the servants and the cook go, some time back. I had to have something to do. Madge is upstairs. She's waiting for you, darling. She's been fussing and primping all day . . . long before the verdict came in. She never doubted you. Never once."

Jeff walked across the living room to the music corner, where the grand piano stood. He let his fingers run up and down the keyboard in the manner of an orchestra leader, calling his band together er after a break. He kept watching the door.

Madge came through it slowly. Madge, at eighteen, was the loveliest girl he had ever seen. She was slim and willowy, with a figure meant for costuming by Dior. Her features were intended for permanent preservation on canvas by competent artists and for immediate enjoyment on magazine covers. She should have had young men standing in line, but she discouraged them. She was a strange girl—she needed him and she always would.

She kept moving toward him, like a scene out of a play where the heroine crosses the stage with that swing-legged actress gait. Then she was suddenly a young girl again. She broke into a run that sent her fluffed-out skirt flying in the breeze she created.

She placed a warm finger across his lips, motioned with her head toward the piano. Neither had uttered a sound so far. Now they sat down on the bench and began to play. Softly at first, and then with more abandon until they were in the middle of Rachmaninoff's Prelude in C# Minor and the music resounded through the house. She stopped abruptly and threw her arms around him.

"Now everything's all right, Daddy. Everything's so damned right I hurt inside, being appreciative. Stan's a louse and a stinker. I would have brained him with that brass vase in the hall if Mother hadn't stopped me. Don't feel bad about him, Daddy. He isn't worth it."

"So long as I have you and your mother," he said. "You're playing better than you used to, Madge."

"I've been practicing," she said, with a winning smile. "That's all I had to do. I swore I wouldn't. go out on any dates while you were locked up. I practiced and practiced . . ."

"They let me use the old upright in the jail auditorium now and then. Kept me from rusting out. Your mother's getting dinner. How about some Chopin—for her."

Madge touched the keys, threw back her head and began to play. Jeff joined in. He closed his eyes lightly, wrapped in the music that swelled and filled the house again. It was a silly idea, because they didn't need the money, but he was sure he and Madge could have been a success on the concert stage. In the next instant, he wondered how he could have been such a fool as to let Corinne get away with it. There'd been no intention on his part to bring her to the lake, but he'd phoned the office that morning, and asked her to send him a manuscript he could work on, in the isolated seclusion of this resort.

She'd brought it in person, flying up and bringing along hiking shorts and a bathing suit. He'd been lonely, she'd always been attractive to him, and after they had a couple of drinks in the lounge, he registered her as his wife. She'd also brought along that silly camera and insisted on taking snaps.

Four weeks later, early one rainy evening, she'd been found sitting in a corner chair in the large lobby of the apartment house where she lived with her sister. Someone had shot her through the side of the head.

Suddenly, he didn't want to play Chopin any more.

After dinner, he, Lydia, and Madge made plans. They'd go, within the week, on an around the world cruise. They'd ask Stan, knowing he'd refuse, but he was their son and they had to make the gesture. They'd stay away six months. Maybe this foul business would dissipate by then, so they could lead normal lives once more.

The next afternoon there were papers to be signed at the office. They could have sent them, but Jeff had an idea he was deliberately summoned there because it would be embarrassing for him. They were all making a fetish of Corinne's aloofness, her outward shell of propriety, her absolute classic beauty. He'd found the shrew that lay beneath that facade, and he'd hated and feared her. Corinne hadn't gone on the make for a few nights' diversion. She wanted him and all he owned.

He didn't look at Molly, back of the newsstand; he brushed by Tommy, the elevator starter, and wondered how many of the solemn-faced people in the elevator knew who he was. Those who didn't would certainly find out after he left the car.

He signed the necessary documents, but refused to look at Bob Shannon because he didn't want to be placed in the position of having to beg for a nod or a smile of recognition. He left as promptly and discreetly as possible.

At home, the doorbell brought Madge to the head of the curving staircase off the reception hall, but Lydia got to the door first. She found a mousy-looking, mousy-acting woman standing on the porch, clutching a wrinkled, brown paper bag against her flat chest. Lydia recognized her as Nell Cameron, the plain, unattractive sister of the lovely and dead Corinne.

Nell must have been about forty but dressed like someone of sixty. She had pipe-stem legs and scrawny shoulders, and her measurements would have made connoisseurs of the subject believe they were dealing with a hatrack and not a woman. She possessed a whining, little voice and an abject manner which actually made her appear to be constantly grovelling.

Lydia had seen her in the witness chair, cringing before the jury and the lawyers. It was no act, but she made it look like one.

"I'm sorry," Lydia said, "my husband isn't home and if he were, I doubt he'd wish to see you."

"It's you I came to see," Nell said. "I got to see you because I'll go to the newspapers if you don't let me in."

"What newspapers?" Lydia asked, and there was no apprehension in her, for Jeff had been acquitted and he couldn't be harmed again.

"All of them. Please . . . you won't like it if I go."

"Come in," Lydia said. "I fail to see how you can harm us any further, Miss Cameron."

She led Nell into the living room. Neither of them thought to look up at the staircase landing where Madge stood watching.

Nell settled herself on the edge of a hard chair, preferring that to a softer one. She removed a rather battered-looking green-painted combination candlestick holder and ash tray from the paper bag. It was a hideous ceramic composition.

"I swore in court that Corinne told me she and Mr. Baron had been together. Your husband said I was a liar, and I guess the jury believed him because they let him go, but I was telling the truth. I can prove it."

A small shiver ran through Lydia. "Then why didn't you, in court?"

"I only found this a little while ago. You see, Corinne always stole something from every hotel, or motel, she ever stayed at. You know—book matches, soap, towels, shoe shine rags. If it had the name of the hotel on it, she took it as a memento. She loved mementos. The candlestick holder was in her old trunk, as if she wanted to hide it, and when I found it, I knew."

"You're not making a great deal of sense," Lydia warned her, but it *was* sense. Horrible, brutal, chilling sense.

"I can't talk well. I'm not fluent. Anyway, you can see the name of the lodge on the ash tray or candlestick. It says Birch Tree Inn, and I heard of it and J just went there. I flew. It was the first time in my life I flew. I was scared. I won't get into a plane again, but I was in a hurry. Your husband was at the Birch Tree Inn last year and so was Corinne. I showed her picture up there and they remembered her. Everybody remembered Connie, she was so beautiful. I guess that's all I need to go to the newspapers. Oh yes, he signed the register as man and wife. That was on June 12th and 13th. You weren't with him, Mrs. Baron, and don't lie and say you were. They'd know up there. They remember Corinne."

Lydia stood up abruptly. "Please go now."

"You understand why I have to tell the newspapers," Nell said. "When your husband was let go, that made me out to be a liar and I was telling the truth. I want everybody to know that."

"You may do precisely what you wish," Lydia said. "Just go. Please . . . get out of this house."

Nell made a hurried exit, closing the door very, very softly behind her because she hated doors that slammed. On the landing, Madge turned away, fluffing out her blond hair, tossing her pretty head as if she'd heard nothing new or surprising.

Lydia packed a bag with essentials and took some money from the bedroom wall safe. She called Stan's hotel from the bedroom phone and told him she'd meet him and to get her a room for an indefinite stay. She draped the mink over her shoulders, purposely and deliberately refused to check her appearance in any of the mirrors, and walked out into the corridor. She knocked at Madge's room. There was no answer. Lydia turned the knob and discovered the door was locked.

"Very well, Madge," she called through the door. "I suppose you heard what went on. I hardly expected you'd come with me. That's why I didn't ask. You may tell your father why I've left him and joined Stan. I'm very sorry all this happened, because none of it is your fault, but I cannot remain here. I'll get in touch with you."

Something substantial and hard hit the inner side of the door. Something thrown in high, vicious rage. Lydia picked up her bag and hurried out of the house to the garage where her own car was waiting. As she drove away, she looked up at Madge's room and thought she saw the curtain fall back. Lydia gave herself the consolation of a choked sob of misery before she settled down to drive.

Jeff returned at six-thirty to find the dining room table set for two, with candlelight, thick steaks, and french fries. Madge wore a black evening gown which gave her a startingly adult appearance. It wasn't cut for modesty, but then, nothing Madge ever did was modest. She wouldn't wear a gown like this to impress, but to shock. And not the boys, but the women.

"Mother's gone." Madge sat down at the table. "She deserted us, and who gives a damn anyway! Daddy, did you fall in love with Corinne?"

He stared at her. "What are you talking about? Mother deserted . . . did I love Corinne. . . ?"

"Nell Cameron was here. She brought proof you and Corinne stayed together at some cozy little nook called the Birch Tree Inn.

Oh, it's all right with me, Dad. Corinne was beautiful. Compared to her, mother's an old cow."

Jeff's lips compressed and he knew if he ate the steak, it would wind up an indigestible bolus in his stomach. He pushed the plate away.

"I was afraid of that," he said. "I depended on the isolation of the place, but in this age, there is no isolation. No, I did not fall in love with Corinne. It was one of those rotten things . . ."

"I'm not hungry either," Madge said "Let's play the piano and talk, like we used to. And Daddy, please don't worry about my leaving you. I wouldn't—even if you were the original Bluebeard with seventy wives. It's a wonderful evening for some Rachmaninoff. That's how I feel, big and loud and brutal. Come on, Dad."

She took his hand and would not be denied. They seated themselves and began to play. Madge, with unleashed enthusiasm; Jeff; unable to match her angry style. His mind was too occupied with thoughts of his broken home, his problematical future. He heard the doorbell dimly and knew Madge jumped up as if she expected someone to call. He kept his eyes closed for a few seconds and then wondered if it might be Lydia, come back to him. His eyes opened wide, but the living room was empty. He could hear voices. It wasn't Lydia so he closed his eyes again and continued to play. He was deep in a world of despair; a man aware that infractions of a moral code have their punishment. A man knowing he had thrown away the good life he'd been born to, grown up with, and then commanded. All for a girl with shell-like skin, a graceful figure, a beautiful face, and a cunning brain dictating to a greedy nature.

"You wanted me to come?" she said, and the blackness cleared and Nell Cameron stood beside the piano, scared, but defiant. Jeff got to his feet.

"I didn't want you here," he said. "Get out."

"But you phoned . . ."

"I did not phone," he said coldly. "You've caused enough trouble . . ."

"I'm sorry, Mr. Baron. I'm very sorry, but you made trouble for me too. You killed my sister. My lovely sister, and you're not going to be made to pay for it. And you did telephone . . . or told your daughter to."

Jeff's startled expression frightened her and she shrank away from him. "Yes, she did call," Nell insisted. "She let me in too . . . just now. She said she'd be with me . . . in . . . a . . . couple of . . . minutes . . ."

She kept speaking as Madge approached, but her mind wasn't on what she said. Her eyes were not on Madge either, but only on the big, blue-black automatic Madge held negligently. The muzzle was pointed down, the sight edge of the barrel resting lightly against her thigh as she walked with that slow, easy grace of hers.

Jeff sat down. He motioned to Nell. "Have a chair, Miss Cameron. Please . . ."

Nell backed away from Madge. She still hadn't lifted her eyes from the gun. Madge idly raised the weapon and gestured with it toward a large, leather-covered chair placed against the wall not far from the piano.

"Sit there," Madge said. "It'll be easier for me to shoot you."

Hysteria hadn't yet reached Nell's voice, though her mouth was slack and her eyes panicky. "Please . . . please . . . don't shoot me. I won't go to the newspapers. It don't make much difference if your father don't pay for killing Corinne. It don't make no difference any more. She's dead! You understand she's dead, and she can't be hurt anymore so I don't care. Please don't shoot me."

"You'll be all right, Miss Cameron," Jeff said. "Madge, come sit with me."

Madge placed the big gun on top of the grand, well out of Jeff's reach, he noted. Then she fluffed out her gown a bit and sat down as if she were to play a large and appreciative audience. Her hands slammed down on the keys. The music crashed through the house. Nell jumped, but settled back, her face a pasty mask of fear.

Jeff joined Madge and the music was heavy and somber, mostly improvisations, now and then shifting to Rachmaninoff and his doleful, Russian mood. It wasn't pleasant music, but they had a captive audience.

It was music to die by, Jeff thought, and he gradually swung into a quieter theme. He forced her to follow him. He always had. He swept grandly into Mozart, held there, then eased into Chopin, lighter and more fluid. Madge hardly realized she was playing softly, gently, and a slow smile came over her face.

Jeff wanted to wipe away the perspiration that formed and beaded on his face. His mouth was dry and he wanted a drink. He was a man who rarely drank, but he wanted one now. The taller, stronger, and stiffer the drink the better, but he never stopped playing. By the music, he was bringing Madge out of her murderous, black mood. For awhile, he didn't think it possible, but he'd accomplished it. Now, if he could only hold her there. Keep her nerves and her mood bright. Then . . . maybe . . . he might be able to save Nell Cameron's life.

Madge slowly closed her eyes while she played and the enchantment of the music held her. Then Nell made her mistake. She watched Madge close her eyes, waited a moment, and got up softly. Jeff wanted to shout to her to sit down, to stay put and not move an inch, but he couldn't call out and he couldn't stop playing to signal with his hands. All he could do was silently mouth the words of warning which Nell didn't grasp.

Nell tiptoed away from the piano, moving faster and faster. Madge simply kept the fingers of her left hand moving nimbly over the keys, while her right hand calmly, almost idly, picked up the automatic. The safety was off. She aimed it and fired.

Jeff froze for a second, not daring to move. Nell's screech rivaled the blare of the gun and, unlike the explosion of the weapon which was over quickly, she kept yelling. She'd fallen flat on her face and her legs were kicking at the rug, while her fingers clawed at it. She kept up the frantic yowling.

Madge said, "Daddy, will you make that silly woman stop her caterwauling? I aimed way over her head."

Jeff nodded, mopped his face and walked casually to where Nel' was now moaning. He helped her up and it was obvious that she hadn't been hit. He glanced at Madge and saw something on her face which made him lead Nell back to the same chair. She sat down, trembling.

Madge said, "Miss Cameron, if you try that again, you'll be a few minutes younger at your death than you will be if you behave yourself. Daddy . . . I want to keep playing. I'm sure Miss Cameron enjoys the music."

He sat down and she began again with the heavy stuff— heavy and loud and filled with the portent of destruction. The automatic lay on top of the piano again, a bit closer to Jeff and he eyed it speculatively. Madge caught the direction of his glance and pushed the gun away with an amused smile.

"Let's work up to it, Daddy," she said. "Miss Cameron has to die. If we don't kill her, she'll go to the newspapers and this whole miserable business will start all over again."

"No!" Nell called out shrilly. "No . . ."

"Shut up!" Jeff shouted harshly. "Keep your mouth closed!"

Nell pressed her body back in the big chair as if she wanted to get lost in it. Madge hadn't stopped playing, but her touch was lighter so their voices could be heard. Now she hit the keys with an impassioned violence and Jeff joined her. He played with her, beyond her. He'd never played like this in his life. The music filled the house with such violence he thought the sound of it might nev-

er go away. They were playing notes again. There was rhythm, but too much wildness for theme. He glanced at her. She was staring straight ahead. A vein in her lovely neck was throbbing. He said something, purposefully low, and she looked at him and shook her head to indicate she hadn't heard.

Deliberately now, he lowered the volume of his playing, drifted into something softer, more soothing, and she followed, without realizing he was deliberately leading her this way.

He said, "Madge, baby, we can't take that trip around the world. Not yet. Not for a little while. I want you to see a doctor."

"If you say so," she agreed dreamily. "You know best, Daddy. You know I killed Corinne, don't you?"

"Yes," he said. "I know."

"I was sure you did. That day —that rainy day, I was beside myself. I hate rain and gloom. I wanted to talk to you, to see you, so I went to your office and I was outside your door after hours, while Corinne threatened you. I heard her say if you didn't divorce mother, she'd make mother divorce you. I knew she was making you very unhappy so I took a taxi home and got the gun. Then I drove my own car to the apartment house where Corinne lived."

"Yes, Madge," he said, and he made the music soft and low, and sweet, improvising mostly, not being able to keep his mind on composition. She followed his lead and she was smiling contentedly.

"I waited there. You brought her in, under an umbrella, remember? I didn't think you'd have anything more to do with her. But you were still angry and she laughed at you. I was there, hiding. I heard it all. After you left, I called Corinne over and she was very angry with me. She said I was a spoiled brat and she'd fix that. So I showed her the gun and I told her nobody could hurt my father. Then I shot her."

"I saw you come out of the building," Jeff said. "I thought you might have . . . done something. I went back in and saw her and I ran away. But someone saw me leaving. Someone who wasn't absolutely certain. That saved me."

"I wouldn't have let them send you to prison," she said.

"It was wrong, Madge." His fingers barely touched the keys and she played quietly, wholly relaxed. "I let them arrest me because I didn't want anything to happen to you. I was going to take you away, but I think we'd better wait. You know it was wrong to kill Corinne, don't you?"

"It was also wrong to make you unhappy and that's what she did."

"Yes . . . yes . . . that's quite true, but it isn't the same as shooting someone. You meant well, darling. Whatever you did, you did for me. There was no selfishness in it, but we can't go on carrying this awful secret with us, Madge. Look what it's already done! Stan ran away. Your mother went off. Now you want to make it worse by killing Miss Cameron."

"That's right," Madge said cheerfully.

"I want you to be kind and generous and let Miss Cameron go. Will you do that for me?"

As he spoke, he stopped playing and slowly reached out his right hand for the automatic. She didn't try to stop him. He slipped the gun in his pocket and nodded curtly at Nell. She got up slowly, walked to the piano and looked at

MERCURY **PUBLICATIONS**

Madge who sat with her arms extended, her fingers on the silent keys, her neck muscles tight as a drum.

Nell put out a hand as if to touch Madge, but obeyed Jeff's quick shake of the head. She walked out quietly and unhurriedly. Jeff put his arm around his daughter.

"Good girl," he said. "We'll call Dr. Norton now. He'll help you and so will I. After awhile, we'll take a long trip. We've a great deal to atone for, and the time to begin is now. I'm as much to blame as you."

"I thought it was so right to kill her." Madge looked at him wonderingly.

"I know you did."

"Will you . . . be able to visit me and . . . shall we be able to play our duets again? I wouldn't mind if . . . we could do that."

"We'll manage it," he said. "Come on now . . . let's make that phone call."

They walked slowly from the piano and across the living room. She slipped her arm about him and looked up at him, smiling sunnily. He smiled back.

It wasn't much of a smile.

www.ingramcontent.com/pod-product-compliance
Lightning Source LLC
Chambersburg PA
CBHW020147180626
46810CB00004B/1770